More Than Friends

Cedar River Daydreams

Other Books by Judy Baer

More Than Friends

Judy Baer

BETHANY HOUSE PUBLISHERS
MINNEAPOLIS, MINNESOTA 55438
A Ministry of Bethany Fellowship, Inc.

More Than Friends
Judy Baer

All scripture quotations are taken from *The Everyday Bible, New Century Version,* copyright © 1987, 1988 by Word Publishing, Dallas, Texas 75039.
Used by permission.

Library of Congress Catalog Card Number 92–73062

ISBN 1–55661–298-2

Published by Bethany House Publishers
A Ministry of Bethany Fellowship, Inc.
6820 Auto Club Road, Minneapolis, Minnesota 55438

Printed in the United States of America

For Serena, Kirsten,
Barb, and Sandy.
May the robin keep flying
for a thousand years.

JUDY BAER received a B.A. in English and Education from Concordia College in Moorhead, Minnesota. She has had over nineteen novels published and is a member of the National Romance Writers of America, the Society of Children's Book Writers and the National Federation of Press Women.

Two of her novels, *Adrienne* and *Paige*, have been prizewinning bestsellers in the Bethany House SPRINGFLOWER SERIES (for girls 12–15). Both books have been awarded first place for juvenile fiction in the National Federation of Press Women's communications contest.

We hold these truths to be self-evident, that all men are created equal.

—Thomas Jefferson

"Love your enemies. Pray for those who hurt you."

Matthew 5:44

I have a dream that little children will one day live in a nation where they will be judged not by the color of their skin but by the content of their character.

—Dr. Martin Luther King

Chapter One

Lexi burst into Todd's house without knocking and moved through the front entry into the Winston's kitchen. Her eyes sparkled and her cheeks were flushed an attractive pink. Lexi's hair was pulled loosely away from her face, held back by a thick ribbon. She wore an over-sized sweatshirt, dark leggings and black leather ballet-type slippers. She hurried to the table where her friends were sitting.

Lexi's boyfriend, Todd Winston, was busy sketching on a note pad but looked up to give her a broad smile. "You're late. We've been waiting for you."

At the far end of the table, Egg McNaughton was spreading peanut butter on crackers. One by one, he popped the crackers into his mouth, and gave a little sigh of satisfaction after each mouthful. As he swallowed, a blissful look settled over his features.

"Hi, Lexi," he mumbled, spraying cracker crumbs through the air.

"Ewww, gross, Egg!" Binky yelped. "Keep your mouth shut while you eat." His sister was sitting at Egg's left, painting Jennifer Golden's fingernails neon pink.

"We're going to do my toenails next," Jennifer said, greeting Lexi. She stuck her left hand in the air. "What do you think of the color? Great, huh? It goes perfectly with the new T-shirt I got yesterday."

"Your fingernails look like jellybeans," Egg commented, gazing hungrily at the tips of Jennifer's fingers.

"Keep eating those crackers, Egg," Jennifer ordered. "You're obviously not full yet."

"That thing will never fly." The statement drew Lexi's attention to the other side of the table.

"Sure it will. Watch."

A paper plane sailed over Lexi's shoulder and landed on the floor behind her.

"See? I told you so," Matt Windsor said triumphantly. He pushed away from the table to retrieve his paper airplane.

Anna Marie Arnold made a face and busied herself making some fine-tuning adjustments on her own paper plane. "I don't see how you got something folded that badly to fly at all, Matt."

"It's all in the aerodynamics. You're too worried about how your plane looks. You got to know how to fold so it will fly."

Belatedly, Lexi noticed that the Winston kitchen floor was covered with paper airplanes. She hid a smile and studied her friends as they sat around the table.

Todd's wheat-blond hair was combed away from his face and he wore a pale blue cotton knit sweater that did something incredible for his eyes. Matt wore a black T-shirt that made his already dark, brooding good looks even more apparent.

Anna Marie looked as though she'd gained a pound or two, Lexi noted happily. She had to work hard to keep her weight near that of her pre-anorexia days.

Binky looked even more worried than usual as she applied a final coat of polish to Jennifer's hand.

"You've got to quit reaching for the sunflower seeds, Jennifer," Binky commanded. "Otherwise we're going to get this goop all over everything. Hold still. I'm almost done."

"You said that half an hour ago," Jennifer retorted. "You're never going to be a beautician, Binky, unless you speed up."

"Who said I wanted to be a beautician?"

Even in her haste and excitement, Lexi had to laugh. The conversation was off-the-wall and fragmented—as usual.

"What's with you? What's so funny?" Jennifer turned her attention from the top of Binky's lowered head to Lexi.

"I have good news." Lexi sank into a straight-backed kitchen chair.

Without comment, Egg handed her a peanut butter-covered cracker and a glass.

Lexi poured herself some juice and took a bite of the cracker. "Actually, I have absolutely marvelous, wonderful news."

"You must have found a hundred-dollar bill under your pillow," Todd suggested.

"Or a manicurist who can do all ten nails without messing the first nine up before she's finished." Jennifer gave Binky a cross look.

"You've built a better airplane," Anna Marie said. "One that flies farther than these silly things do."

"Aren't you going to ask me about my news?" Lexi demanded. "Binky, there are enough coats of paint on Jennifer's fingernails already. Pay attention! Something wonderful is going to happen!"

"Okay, spill it, Lexi."

"You know how much I talk about Grover's Point."

"Sure we do," Binky said. "That's because it's where you grew up. You moved to Cedar River from there."

"My very best friend from Grover's Point is coming to visit!" Lexi clapped her hands together and her eyes gleamed with delight. "Can you believe it? My friend Ashleigh is coming to town."

"Soon?"

"Very soon. Ashleigh's father is a guest speaker at the Community College. She didn't tell me all the details when she called, but she said he would be in town for a few days setting up a new program. While he's here, Ashleigh is going to stay with me. Isn't that great?"

"We'll finally get to meet one of your friends from Grover's Point," Jennifer said. "After all the stories I've heard, I feel I should know them already."

"Does she get to miss school to come here?" Binky asked.

"She's gotten permission to be absent a couple of days. She'll be going to school with me. Her father decided it would be a learning experience."

"I'm glad she's coming," Todd said. "It will be good to connect a face with the name and stories."

"I have all your Grover's Point friends mixed up," Jennifer admitted. "I can't remember anything about Ashleigh."

"Tell us about her," Binky commanded. "We should know something about her before she gets here. Is she the one who shared a horse costume with you?"

Lexi burst into laughter. "Yes, she is. I forgot that I told you about that."

"You didn't tell me," Egg protested.

"Or me," said Matt.

"Tell them, Lexi. It's the funniest story ever."

Lexi's face was a bright pink. "I don't think I want to bring this up. It's too embarrassing."

"Then I'll tell them," Binky said. "Lexi and her friend Ashleigh went to a costume party as a horse. Before they went, they got into a big fight over who would be the front end of the horse and who would be the back."

"A horse?" Todd laughed in disbelief. "Lexi, is she telling the truth?"

"Well ... they were giving prizes for the most original costume. Ashleigh and I thought we had a great idea. We just hadn't worked out who would be the front of the horse before we were ready to leave for the party."

"Let me guess." Matt chuckled. "You both wanted to be the front and neither of you wanted to be the back."

"Exactly. The front end of the horse got to stand up. The back end had to bend over for the whole evening. What was worse, if you were the back of the horse, you couldn't see where you were going. You just had to tag along with the front. It was awful."

"Are you saying you were the back end of the horse?"

"It wasn't an easy decision," Lexi admitted, "but we finally resolved the problem."

"How?" Egg asked.

"We decided that whoever was willing to wear the

back end of the custom would get two-thirds of the prize money."

But what if you didn't win a prize?"

"Then the front end of the horse had to *pay* the back end of the horse from her allowance." Lexi giggled and blushed. "Ashleigh's allowance was bigger than mine. She wanted to avoid the back end of that costume so badly that she agreed to one third of the prize money, or paying me from her allowance."

"Well? What happened? Did you win, or did she have to pay you?"

"We won the grand prize! Not only did we win the prize money, but we also received a free dinner for two and we got our picture in the *Grover's Point* paper." Lexi giggled. "Of course, no one could tell who we were. I was grateful for that—considering the 'position' I was in."

Jennifer, Binky, Anna Marie, and Egg laughed out loud. Todd and Matt shook their heads in amazement.

Jennifer snapped her fingers. "I remember another story about Ashleigh. Is she the one who talked you in to cutting your hair?"

"Yes." Lexi put her hands to her head. "Oh, what a mess that was! Ashleigh told me that not only would I look great with my hair short but also that she could cut it for me."

"How did that turn out?" Anna Marie questioned.

"Just awful. Ashleigh thought she'd learned to cut hair by reading an article in a magazine. My hair wouldn't have looked any worse if I'd stuck it in a blender and turned it on. It was so choppy and uneven that even my mother burst out laughing when she saw me."

"Lexi, I can't believe you'd allow someone to do that to you."

"Ashleigh's pretty convincing." Lexi grinned. "Unfortunately, my hair looked terrible for weeks. Mom took me to a salon and we tried to get it straightened out, but even the beauty operator said she'd never seen anything quite like it."

When the laughter subsided, Lexi continued. "And that wasn't the worst of it! Ashleigh had promised that I'd get to cut *her* hair when she was done cutting mine. After she saw what mine looked like, she wouldn't let me touch hers. She said she'd decided she liked long hair better than short."

"I can hardly wait to meet this girl," Egg said. "She sounds great to me."

"Ashleigh and I have had some really fun times together. When we were little, we ran a lemonade stand all summer long. We wasted more of my mom's sugar and lemons than we ever made enough money to pay for. Of course, one year we did have a good idea. Too bad it didn't work out."

"What was that?"

"Ashleigh and I decided that it wasn't working out to charge ten cents a glass for lemonade. We'd have to sell at least twenty glasses in order for each of us to make a dollar. We liked our lemonade sweet so we used at least two dollars worth of sugar before we even got the pitcher of lemonade to the sidewalk."

"So, what was your idea?"

"We decided that instead of selling twenty glasses of lemonade for ten cents a glass, we would just sell *two* glasses of lemonade for two dollars a glass!"

"Who was going to pay two dollars for a glass of lemonade?"

"No one!"

"I love it. This is great," Matt said. "Tell us more!"

"There's nothing much to tell, unless you want to hear about the mud pie stand."

"You tried to sell mud pies?" Binky screeched.

"For three years. When we hadn't sold any in all that time, we figured that we didn't have a very saleable product. Before we closed our stand, Ashleigh went on a big marketing campaign. Whenever anyone would come by in a car or on a bike, she'd stand in front of our little mud pie stand with a big smile on her face, and demonstrate how tasty and nutritious our mud pies were."

"You mean she ate them?"

"When Mom caught us, she nearly had a stroke," Lexi admitted. "She made Ashleigh go inside and eat a piece of toast and drink a glass of milk. Then she gave Ashleigh a toothbrush and made her brush her teeth over and over again. Mother was really upset, but it didn't hurt Ashleigh. Her parents were a lot more calm about that escapade. They said there were bound to be vitamins and minerals in mud too."

Matt was laughing so hard that he nearly fell off his chair. "I've got to meet this girl. She sounds great."

"Eating mud pies. Ewww." Binky made a face.

"Mud pies weren't the only thing Ashleigh tried to sell. Once she convinced me to gather all my old toys. We had a rummage sale on the street corner and sold them to neighborhood children."

"You sold your toys?" Binky gasped.

"Ashleigh thought we could use the money to buy new ones. Unfortunately, we didn't price the toys very wisely. We didn't even make enough money for one trip to the toy store."

"It sounds like you and Ashleigh have had some great times," Binky exclaimed.

" . . . and some bad ones," Egg added.

"We have," Lexi agreed. "We've shared everything, including the chicken pox and the stomach flu. One of the reasons I felt so sad when I moved to Cedar River was that I had to leave Ashleigh behind. Fortunately, all of you helped make the transition easier."

"Ahhh, isn't that sweet?" Jennifer said.

Lexi playfully poked her in the arm. "You will absolutely love Ashleigh. She's so much fun. I can hardly wait for you to meet her."

Todd stood up and stretched. "I, for one, am very anxious to meet this girl. I have a lot of questions to ask her. Since you didn't grow up in Cedar River, we don't know much about you when you were young, Lexi. Maybe Ashleigh can tell us a few things about you."

"Some secrets," Binky said, growing excited. "Maybe Ashleigh can tell us about the times Lexi goofed up."

"Great idea," Jennifer agreed. "After all, Lexi's been practically 'perfect' since she's moved to Cedar River."

"She's hardly gotten into any trouble at all."

"It would be nice to have some 'dirt' on her," Binky said jokingly. "That way we could make sure that Lexi's human like the rest of us."

Lexi took the teasing in stride.

"By the way, when is Ashleigh going to arrive?" Matt asked.

"She and her dad will be arriving Friday night."

"Isn't there a basketball game here Friday

night?" Matt wondered aloud.

"Yes. It's perfect." Lexi clapped her hands with pleasure. "Ashleigh can meet all of you at the game. You'll love her. I just know it." Lexi pushed herself away from the table and glanced at the clock on the wall. "I've got to go. I'd better clean my room. Ashleigh will need somewhere to put her clothes. She won't think the dust bunnies under my bed are nearly as funny as my brother, Ben, does."

Jennifer whistled through her teeth. "Ashleigh must be very special! After all," she added slyly, "Lexi doesn't clean her room for just anyone!"

Chapter Two

By Friday afternoon, Lexi was so excited about seeing Ashleigh that she was practically giddy. Ruth Nelson caught up with Lexi in the hallway after the final bell.

"What are you laughing about?" Lexi asked when she saw Ruth's big smile.

"You. I don't think I've ever seen you so excited."

"You've heard my friend Ashleigh is coming from Grover's Point, haven't you?"

"Everybody in the entire school has heard about her at least once—probably twice."

Lexi blushed. "I'm being a little silly, I know, but Ashleigh is so much fun and we were so close that I can't help it."

"It's all right, I understand. You're acting the same way I'll act when my parents come home. There'll be so much to talk about I won't know where to begin."

Ruth's parents were missionaries. While they were overseas, Ruth was staying with her aunt in Cedar River. Ruth had a hearing handicap that made it difficult for her at first, but now she had good friends in Cedar River and was well accepted by everyone.

Lexi nodded. "I'm so excited I could burst!"

Todd walked up to the two girls. "Need a ride home?"

"You bet. Maybe Ashleigh will arrive early."

"How about you, Ruth?"

"I'm staying after school. I have a meeting in the Home Ec. room."

"Let's go, Todd." Lexi pulled at his arm.

Todd laughed helplessly. "I wish you were that anxious to see me, Lexi."

"I'm always glad to see you. I'd be especially glad to see you if it'd been months and months since we'd been together. But since I'm seeing you right now and Ashleigh might be waiting at my place . . ."

"All right, all right. I get it. Quit talking and start driving, right?"

Once they were on their way to the Leighton house, Lexi gave a small sigh and turned toward Todd. "You think I'm out of my mind, don't you, behaving the way I am about Ashleigh's visit?"

"No, I don't. In fact, I think you're lucky."

"Really?"

"It's not very often that people make friends that last a lifetime. My mom says casual friends will always enter and leave your life, but few will be with you over the years. I assume *now* that Egg, Matt, and the other guys will be my buddies forever, but who knows?"

"I have been lucky," Lexi said. "I thought my heart was going to shatter when Dad told me we were leaving Grover's Point so he could open a veterinary clinic in Cedar River. I begged to stay behind and live with Ashleigh and her family. Of course, my parents wouldn't hear of that. Since I've been in Cedar

River, I've met new friends that are equally special. Jennifer, Peggy, Binky, you." Lexi laughed lightly. "The list goes on and on. I guess God really has blessed me, hasn't He?"

"That's another thing my mom says. She believes we should view our friends as gifts from God. If we treat them with special care, they should last forever."

"The Bible says, 'a friend loves you all the time.' That's how I think of Ashleigh—as someone who loves me all the time, no matter what I do."

As they neared her home, Lexi leaned forward. There was an unfamiliar car parked in front of the house. "She's here, Todd! I'm sure that's her dad's new car. She's here!"

Todd pulled up behind the big white car. "Have fun, Lexi."

"Aren't you coming inside to meet her?"

"No. I'll wait until the basketball game tonight. You two will want some time alone together. I have a hunch you have lots to catch up on."

"Are you sure?"

"Tonight will be soon enough, Lexi. Don't worry about it."

"Thanks, Todd. Thanks for understanding."

"That's easy. You're good friends."

"We're *more than* friends. We're practically sisters."

Lexi got out of the car in such haste that she dropped her books on the sidewalk.

Todd chuckled. "Are you this excited when I come to visit you?"

Lexi grinned at him impishly. "Oh, definitely."

Todd laughed and revved his engine. "Get out of here. I'll see you tonight."

Lexi hurried up the sidewalk and mounted the steps to the house. The door was ajar and Lexi could hear voices inside. She left her school books on the small table in the foyer and entered the living room.

Lexi's mother was sitting on the couch, holding a coffee mug in her hand. She was smiling at a tall, dark man standing by the fireplace. He, too, held a coffee cup and leaned casually against the mantel. He was an imposing figure in his dark brown western-cut suit, eel skin boots, bolo tie, and impressive display of silver and turquoise jewelry. Lexi was taken aback for a moment to realize how very handsome he was with his straight black hair and dark narrow eyes.

"Hello, Mr. White Eagle," Lexi greeted him. "It's so nice to see you again."

The man's eyes crinkled pleasantly in greeting. "Hello, Lexi. How are you?"

"Where's . . ."

A loud whoop from the dining room diverted Lexi's attention. The beautiful Indian girl came running through the doorway, her hair flying and her eyes shining.

"It's you, Lexi. It's really you!"

"Ashleigh!"

"You look great!" Ashleigh said, studying Lexi carefully at arms length. "I love the way you're wearing your hair."

"And you're prettier than ever," Lexi responded.

Lexi's statement was true. Ashleigh White Eagle was a stunning girl with long dark hair, dark eyes which were slightly slanted, high cheek bones, and a wide, even smile. She was wearing her trademark feather and porcupine quill earrings just as she always had in Grover's Point.

More than once Lexi and Ashleigh had joked about how two people who looked so different could be so similar. Ashleigh and Lexi embraced and did a giddy, silly dance around the room.

"You've gotten taller."

"Your hair has grown."

"Where did you get those shoes? I love them."

"We'll have to go shopping while you're here. We have a great mall."

"Mall? That word is music to my ears. You know how it is in Grover's Point. Three stores and a catalog; that's our shopping."

"You're right, but I thought I was going to die when I had to leave. How is everyone?"

"Just fine. They all said to tell you hello. I've got a whole suitcase full of letters for you." Ashleigh's eyes twinkled. "I've even got a few for Ben, from some of his old girlfriends. How's Ben doing?"

"Still a sweetie and breaking hearts." Lexi smiled proudly. "He's going to the Academy for the Handicapped. Everybody loves him. They can't help it."

"He's certainly not short on charm," Ashleigh agreed. "I can hardly wait to see him. I suppose he's all grown up."

Lexi touched the delicate earring in one of Ashleigh's ears. "They're beautiful. Do you still make your own?"

"Yes, and I brought a pair for you. In fact, I brought several, just in case you wanted to give them to your friends."

Lexi was about to plunge into a whole new conversation when she finally remembered her manners. "Oh, I'm sorry!" She turned to Ashleigh's father who was still leaning against the fireplace watching the girls. "I'm not being very polite. How are you Mr. White Eagle?"

Richard White Eagle and Marilyn Leighton both burst out laughing.

"I wondered how long it would take them to remember we were here," Ashleigh's father said to Lexi's mother. "Quite frankly, I didn't expect it to happen so quickly."

"I thought they'd crossed parents off the list of interesting topics years ago."

"Oh, Mom. I'm really happy to see Mr. White Eagle." Lexi dimpled sweetly. "After all, he's the one who brought Ashleigh here today."

"She's got a point, Richard," Mrs. Leighton said. "Why don't you girls sit down and visit with us for a few minutes? I'll get the coffeepot."

Lexi turned to Ashleigh's father. "It's great of you to let Ashleigh miss school to visit me."

"I could hardly stop her," he said honestly. "Once Ashleigh heard that I was coming to Cedar River, she wouldn't leave me alone for a moment. She begged and pleaded until I promised she could join me."

"Oh, Dad, I wasn't that bad," Ashleigh demurred.

"You certainly made it known that you'd never let me forget it if you couldn't come along."

"And here I am! Isn't it great?"

"What will you be doing at the college, Mr. White Eagle?" Lexi asked. "I was so excited to hear that you were coming that I forgot to ask Ashleigh."

"I'll be kicking off a Native American Studies

program. I have the privilege of being their first guest speaker. Much of my material will be introductory. Since I am a Sioux, I'll be discussing the history of the Sioux and their traditions."

"I hate to admit it," Lexi said, "but I really don't know much about Ashleigh's ancestors. When I think about Ashleigh, she's just . . . well . . . just Ashleigh!"

Mr. White Eagle chuckled. "That's all right, Lexi. Sometimes when people begin to label one another, more harm is done than good. Ashleigh is your friend because of who she is as a person, not what tribe or culture she came from."

"But isn't it careless of me not to know *something* about her heritage?"

"I don't now anything about your ancestors, Lexi. It's something friends take for granted. It only gets in the way when people can't see beyond the color of someone's skin."

"But that doesn't mean I'm not interested. Why not practice your speech on us?"

"My ancestors were nomadic hunters and warriors. One hundred fifty years ago the Sioux nation was very powerful. Its organization is fairly complex, Lexi. There are seven bands within the nation itself which began long ago with the Seven Council fires. Each of the divisions was independent of one another, but met every summer to hold council and make decisions for the entire nation."

I should do some reading about this, Lexi decided.

"The Sioux people had an interest in their own pasts. Though they didn't have a written history, the old men told tales from long ago by the fire in the evenings. That's called an 'oral tradition.' "

"If they didn't write anything down, how did they keep track of time?"

"Rather than *numbering* years as we do now, they gave each year a title. The year was named for an exciting, unusual, or outstanding event. Therefore, if a tribe member wanted to tell you what year he was born, he might say he was born in the Year the Sun Died."

"What did that mean?" Lexi wondered aloud.

"The Year the Sun Died was a year in which there was a solar eclipse."

"It makes sense to me. That's easier than trying to remember what happened in a year like 1927 or 1954." Lexi's interest was piqued. "What did the Sioux do for food?"

"They were hunters. They traveled in small groups over large areas of land. Being nomadic was their way of life."

"That sounds like a lot of hard work."

"The Sioux are a very brave and generous people. They led difficult lives. The bravery of both men and women was essential in order to survive."

"What's more," Ashleigh added, "the Sioux women were industrious. They did quill embroidery and tanned hides to make tepees, moccasins, dresses, and cradles."

"That's really interesting!" Lexi said with enthusiasm. "I should have learned these things before now."

"You're not alone, Lexi," Mr. White Eagle said. "It's surprising how little people know about Native Americans. That's why I'm here. My goal is to spark an interest in learning about my people. We have a beautiful and interesting heritage. Once others study it, they'll become excited about our history."

"Are there many Native Americans in your school, Lexi?" Mrs. Leighton asked.

"Umm . . . not that I know of. There are several Asian, Black, and Mexican kids. I don't pay much attention to the color of anyone's skin. A friend is a friend to me—no matter what color they are."

"I wish everyone felt that way, Lexi. In my years as a teacher, I've seen signs of prejudice that have wounded me deeply. I've come to the conclusion that prejudice springs from fear and misunderstanding. That's why I'm here—to open doors of understanding and acceptance, which until now have been closed. The Native American Studies program at the college will be good for everyone."

Ashleigh poked Lexi in the arm. "Don't get Dad started on this. He can go on for hours and hours about our heritage."

"I think it's interesting," Lexi admitted.

"I can hear all about race relations and Indian history at home. Come on, Lexi. Show me your room. Introduce me to your friends. I want to hear all about your life in Cedar River!"

Mr. White Eagle glanced at Mrs. Leighton. "I don't impress my daughter at all, do I?"

"Can any father or mother really impress their own children?" Mrs. Leighton responded. "We're too familiar."

"I'd better leave before my ego is ruined completely." Mr. White Eagle looked at his watch. "I have a dinner meeting tonight. It seems my daughter is eager for me to leave so she can get on with her visit. Thanks for allowing Ashleigh to stay with you for a few days. We appreciate your hospitality."

Mrs. Leighton rose gracefully from the couch and shook Mr. White Eagle's hand. "Ashleigh is like a daughter to Jim and me," she assured him. "I missed her as much as Lexi did when we first moved to Cedar River. It's wonderful having her in the house again. I've already been grocery shopping and have a supply of her favorite foods."

"Thank you. I'm going, Ashleigh," her father called.

"Don't worry about me at all," Ashleigh said, returning to the living room. "It's going to be great here. Nothing but fun!"

Mr. White Eagle gave Ashleigh a kiss on the top of her head. "I hope there's time for something other than fun, like sleeping, perhaps?"

"I can sleep when I get home!"

"Be good, kitten."

"Oh, Daddy," Ashleigh groaned.

After Mr. White Eagle had disappeared through the door, she rolled her eyes and made a face. "Fathers—they're all alike, aren't they?"

"Your dad's great. He's really sweet," Lexi said.

"I know, but he's also overprotective." Dismissing him, Ashleigh clapped her hands together. "Can you believe it? I'm here—with you—in Cedar River?"

Both girls started to squeal. They grabbed each other by the shoulders and repeated their dance around the room.

Mrs. Leighton shook her head as she headed for the kitchen. "And now the fun begins!"

Chapter Three

Lexi glanced at her wristwatch. "It's six o'clock already? We'd better finish getting ready for the basketball game. I didn't realize how quickly time had passed while we were talking."

"How do I look?" Ashleigh spun on her tiptoes. "Is this all right for a game? Am I overdressed? Underdressed?"

"You're absolutely perfect," Lexi assured her with sincerity. Ashleigh looked wonderful in her slim-cut jeans and white T-shirt, with a navy blue blazer. Her belt and shoes were both a chocolate brown. From her earlobes dangled another pair of the distinctive feather earrings.

Ashleigh had pulled the sides and top of her shiny black hair away from her face and secured it with a strip of beaded leather. As usual, she looked stunning.

When Lexi lived in Grover's Point, she'd taken Ashleigh's looks and heritage for granted. To her, it was no more unusual than that of her friends who were German, Scandinavian, or Italian. Now, after their conversation with Mr. White Eagle, Lexi began to realize that Ashleigh's family had a very special and unique history. She was proud to be her friend.

Ashleigh studied the soft pink nail polish on her nails. "Too much, Lexi? What do you think?" She waggled the tips of her fingers under Lexi's nose.

"Just perfect. As usual. You know that."

"You're good for my ego." Ashleigh looked at Lexi fondly. "I missed you so much when you moved. It was the most miserable time in my life. There I was, in Grover's Point, without a best friend, without the family that I'd practically adopted, without Ben as my 'almost' little brother. It was awful, Lexi."

"I missed you, too." Lexi couldn't even begin to tell her how much. "It took a whole gang of kids to replace you, Ashleigh. My new friends are great, though. I can hardly wait for you to meet them."

"It's Egg I really want to meet," Ashleigh admitted. "After all I've heard about him, I have to see if this character is for real. What kind of guy would decide to put a brick in every toilet, or go on a crazed fitness binge just to impress a girl like Minda?"

"Egg's got a new crush now. Her name is Angela. She's much sweeter than Minda. I'm surprised you even remembered Minda's name."

"How could I forget? Anyone who's caused you that much trouble is unforgettable in my book."

"There are lots of nice people in Cedar River, too."

"Like Todd?" Ashleigh's smile turned sly. "He sounds like a doll to me. Blond hair, blue eyes, broad shoulders." She put her hands over her heart, batted her eyelashes and gave a little sigh.

"Very funny." Lexi was busy tying her shoelaces but decided to throw a pillow across the room at Ashleigh anyway.

"And of course there's Binky. What a great name. And Peggy and Jennifer." Ashleigh turned away from the mirror. "Are you sure I look all right? I don't want to embarrass you or make you feel glad you moved away from Grover's Point."

"You look exactly right," Lexi assured her friend.

"Maybe I should dress up a little more. I brought along a suede skirt. Do you think that would be better?" Ashleigh fussed.

"For a ball game? Don't bother. We'll be climbing up and down the bleachers. Besides, you're a knock-out already."

"You don't look so bad yourself," Ashleigh returned the compliment. "Love that jacket."

"Thanks, I made it myself."

"You're still sewing?"

"When I get the time, which isn't very often anymore. I was working at my dad's veterinary clinic, but he recently hired a lady—Angela's mom—to fill in for me. That should give me a few more hours a week to sew."

"I'm sorry to be worrying so much about how I look. You know I'm not usually like this. My dad has always taught me that it's what's *under* a person's skin that counts; but tonight I feel so insecure. I was your best friend for years and years. Now I have to meet the people who've taken my place."

"No one could ever take your place, Ashleigh. Don't you know that? Besides, my friends don't care what people look like. You could be wearing a parka and swim fins and it wouldn't matter to them. Trust me on this one."

"Okay. If you're sure." Ashleigh pressed her hands to her flat stomach. "I'm nervous! My stomach is growling."

"I don't think it's nerves. I think it's hunger pangs," Lexi diagnosed.

Just then, Mrs. Leighton's voice floated up from the bottom of the stairs. "Girls, are you going to eat? I've got a pizza ready."

"Is that good timing or what?" Lexi said. "Come on. Let's go downstairs."

Mrs. Leighton had the kitchen table set with a red and white checked tablecloth. There was a huge cheese and pepperoni pizza sitting in the middle of the table, cut and ready to eat.

"Hi, Ashleigh," Ben said cheerfully. He was already seated at the table with a big red and white checked napkin tied beneath his chin. "Mom said I couldn't have pizza until you guys were here. Sit down so I can eat."

"Yes, sir." Ashleigh gave Ben a comical little salute.

After prayer, they dug into the pizza with relish. When it was half gone, Ben sighed and rubbed his stomach. "I feel better now."

"Me too," Ashleigh agreed.

Ben studied her intently.

"Do you have a question, Ben?" Ashleigh asked.

"Did you miss me?" he asked.

"Of course I did. It was like losing my little brother when you moved away."

"I missed you too. Do you still have Bart and Betsy?" Ben referred to the pair of mongrel dogs that Ashleigh had adopted.

"No, I'm afraid not. Bart and Betsy went to a farm. They got too big. Now I have a little beagle named Bentley. He's just right for me."

"Bentley the Beagle," Ben rolled the words over his tongue. "Have you seen my bunny yet?"

"No, but I've heard about him. Will you introduce us tomorrow?"

Ben nodded somberly. "I told him about you. He wants to meet you."

"That's very nice of you, Ben."

"Do you still blow bubbles in your milk?" Ben inquired casually.

Ashleigh nearly choked on the pizza crust she was chewing. "Why, Ben, I don't blow bubbles in my milk!"

"Yes, you do. Every time your mom's and dad's backs are turned. I've seen you."

"Who says this boy is handicapped?" Ashleigh turned to Lexi. "He's got a memory that just won't quit."

"I remember lots of things about you, Ashleigh. I remember the time you got your shoes stuck in the mud. They were too gooey to get out, so you just left them in the mud puddle."

"Quiet, Ben."

"And I remember the time you picked all of Mrs. Hanson's tulips and sold them to her at her back door. Mama said we could never do that."

Ashleigh was beginning to blush. "Ben, be quiet."

"And I remember the time you and Lexi made chocolate chip cookies. You ate all the chocolate chips before the cookie dough was done."

"Ben, enough!" both girls said in unison.

Mrs. Leighton ruffled Ben's hair. "I think you have what your sister considers a 'big mouth,' Benjamin."

"Big mouth," Ben echoed in agreement.

"Mom, I'd like to get out of here before Ben gets us into trouble. Can I have the car tonight?"

Mrs. Leighton dug in the pocket of her jeans. "I had a hunch you were going to ask. I checked it out with Dad. He said it was fine. Buckle your seat belts. Don't drive fast. Be home early."

"All parents are alike," Ashleigh commented. "That's exactly what my mother would say." She leaned forward and gave Ben a hug. In turn, he planted a tomatoey kiss on her cheek.

"Come on, Ashleigh," Lexi urged. "You can play with Ben later. Right now we've got to get to the ball game. I can hardly wait for my friends to meet you!"

———————

"Nice school," Ashleigh exclaimed as they drove into the Cedar River High parking lot. "Big."

"Only when compared to the Grover's Point school," Lexi said with a laugh. "It's a good school though. There are some really neat teachers here, like the music instructor, Mrs. Waverly. Mr. Raddis, our history teacher, is good too. Todd says Coach Drummond is one of the best. Of course, we have our share of boring ones too."

Lexi parked the car in the parking lot and led Ashleigh toward the school.

"We'll put our coats in my locker. The bottoms of the bleachers are open and coats slide right through. This way we'll save Egg a trip under the bleachers after the game's over."

"I can hardly wait to meet this Egg guy. He sounds like one of a kind."

"Without a doubt."

Several people greeted Lexi and Ashleigh as they walked down the hallway. Lexi noticed that they all stared curiously at Ashleigh. That was to be expected. Anyone as beautiful as Ashleigh would attract attention.

"There they are." Lexi pointed to the far end of the bleachers. "Up there at the top. Egg is the one trying to stuff an entire red licorice rope into his mouth."

The B-squad game was already in progress. When the first quarter ended, Lexi and Ashleigh made their way to the top bleachers. On the way, they passed Minda.

"Hi, Lexi," Minda greeted her with more friendliness than usual.

Lexi knew why. Minda couldn't keep her eyes off Ashleigh. In the fluorescent light of the gymnasium, her long dark hair gleamed like black gold. Lexi could see Minda eyeing Ashleigh from head to foot and back again. No doubt Minda would have a hundred questions for her later.

"Minda, I'd like you to meet my friend, Ashleigh White Eagle. She's from Grover's Point."

"Hi. Glad to meet you."

After they'd passed, Ashleigh whispered to Lexi, "That's *the* Minda? The one who caused you so much trouble? She doesn't look so bad."

"Minda's mellowing, slowly but surely. By the time we're seniors, we'll probably be best of friends."

"Or college roommates?" Ashleigh added sarcastically.

"Something like that." Lexi rolled her eyes.

They mounted the bleacher steps to the gang's spot. Todd, Egg, and Matt were on the top bleacher. Binky, Peggy, and Jennifer were below them. Lexi knew that Anna Marie, Ruth, and Angela had not planned to come tonight.

"Well, here they are. Hi, guys."

" . . . Uh . . . oh, hi." Egg was staring at Lexi's friend with undisguised interest.

Matt and Todd were doing the same. In fact, Lexi felt as though a thousand pairs of eyes were drilling through both of them. Even the girls were staring intently.

"I'd like you to meet my very dearest friend from Grover's Point, Ashleigh White Eagle. Ashleigh, these are my friends." Lexi ticked off their names. "Jennifer, Binky, Peggy, Todd, Matt, Egg."

Binky gaped, slack-jawed, with a handful of popcorn held halfway to her lips. Jennifer's blue eyes narrowed. Peggy's expression was blatantly curious.

Though Todd and Matt smiled and greeted Ashleigh, Egg just gawked.

Lexi had an uneasy feeling about the way her friends were behaving. She'd expected them to be warm and welcoming. Instead they were behaving as if she and Ashleigh were a new addition to the petting zoo.

"It's nice to meet you, Ashleigh." Egg wiped his hand on the leg of his jeans and stood up to shake her hand.

"Same here," Matt muttered.

"I've been looking forward to meeting you," Todd said politely.

The girls all nodded their heads. "We've heard . . . a little bit . . . about you," Jennifer said.

Lexi was startled at Jennifer's half truth. They'd heard a *lot* about Ashleigh. She'd told her friends everything about her! Why were they acting as though she'd dropped Ashleigh on them unexpectedly? They were too quiet and, if it were possible, too polite.

Suddenly there was a roar from the crowd as the Cedar River team made a three-point basket. Lexi decided to ignore her friends' strange reactions as she and Ashleigh were drawn into the excitement of the game.

Chapter Four

When the A-squad game was over, Lexi sagged against the bleacher seat behind her. "I'm glad that's over. I'm so exhausted I feel like I played the game myself."

"How about celebrating at the Hamburger Shack?" Egg suggested. "Winning a game always makes me hungry."

"Losing a game always makes you hungry."

"Watching a game always makes you hungry."

"*Everything* makes you hungry, Egg."

Egg pulled another licorice rope out of his sack of candy. Binky grabbed it away. "After what you packed away tonight, I'd be surprised if you're hungry for at least a week."

"Where does he put all that food anyway?" Jennifer said in mock disgust. "If I ate like that, I'd weigh two hundred pounds."

"He has a hollow leg. That's what Dad says," Binky informed her.

"Even that hollow leg should be full tonight. Let's go to the Hamburger Shack anyway. I'm sure he can find room for a malt."

"I've got my bike," Matt said, referring to the motorcycle he always rode.

39

"Anybody who wants to can ride with me; I've got my car," Todd said.

"I have my dad's car tonight," Lexi announced proudly. "Ashleigh and I can meet everyone else at the Shack." She looked directly at Peggy, Jennifer, and Binky. "Unless you want to ride with us."

"Um . . . no thanks. I don't think so. I'll go with Todd," Peggy stammered.

Jennifer shook her head. "I'll ride with Matt on his motorcycle."

"We'll meet you there," Binky stated. "I'll ride with Egg and Todd."

Lexi was disappointed. She'd assumed that all three girls would want to ride with her and Ashleigh. It was the perfect opportunity to visit. She sensed that her friends were avoiding them. She didn't understand what was wrong.

"All right." Lexi turned to Ashleigh. "Come on, let's go to the car."

Ashleigh nodded agreeably and descended the steps to the basketball floor. When Lexi turned back to say something to Todd, she was stricken by the expressions on her friends' faces. She saw doubt, confusion, and curiosity, not the pleasure or anticipation she'd expected. Without a word, Lexi turned to hurry after her friend.

As they walked through the halls to the door, Tim Anders came out of the *Cedar River Review* work room.

"Working tonight, Tim? You deserve a reward for that."

Tim laughed as he closed the door. "I had some film to drop off. Don't worry, I'm not that dedicated. Besides, the *Review* always gets out on time whether I work late or not."

Ashleigh stood between Lexi and Tim looking curiously at the boy.

"Tim, I'd like you to meet my friend, Ashleigh White Eagle. Ashleigh is from Grover's Point. She's in town for a few days."

Tim gave Ashleigh a wide, welcoming smile. "Hi, nice to meet you." He stuck out his hand politely and Ashleigh shook it. "We've heard a lot about Grover's Point since Lexi came to town. I'm glad to know it's a real place and not something she imagined."

"Very funny, Tim."

Tim stared at Ashleigh's earrings. "Those earrings are great," he said. "I've never seen anything like them."

"Thank you. I made them myself."

"No kidding?" Tim looked surprised. "That looks difficult."

Lexi smiled to herself. Tim was obviously smitten by Ashleigh's beauty and natural friendliness. He was more animated and less shy than Lexi had ever seen him.

"You're Native American, right?" Tim asked.

"Yes, I am Sioux," Ashleigh said.

"I did a paper for history class on the Sioux Indians. The research was fascinating. They were warriors and hunters, right?"

"True, but they had fun too," Ashleigh said with a laugh. "They played a lot of games and loved competition. You'd think with life as hard as it was, they'd want to take it easy, but they didn't."

"I suppose that kept them primed for whatever might come next. I'm a history buff," Tim admitted. "I have some other questions I'd like to ask you . . ." He seemed to have completely forgotten that Lexi was standing next to them.

"Tim." Lexi poked him on the arm. "We're on our way to the Hamburger Shack."

"I'm sorry. I didn't mean to hog your friend, Lexi. It's just that there's so much I'd like to talk to her about . . ."

"Why don't you meet us there? Then you can ask all the questions you want."

"Sounds great. See you at the Shack." Rather than turn around to walk away, Tim backed down the hall, grinning and waving at Ashleigh. Once he disappeared, Lexi began to giggle.

"What's so funny?" Ashleigh demanded. "He's a sweet guy."

"I think you've made a 'conquest,' Ashleigh. He's crazy about you."

"He's just interested in Native Americans, that's all. I'm impressed by the research he did for his project."

"He's interested in you, too."

"I guess he *was* kind of cute," Ashleigh admitted, wearing a silly grin.

Lexi was delighted that Ashleigh and Tim had met. His energy and enthusiasm made up for the weird way her other friends were behaving.

All the way to the Hamburger Shack, Ashleigh drilled Lexi with questions about Tim.

———

"Todd is already here," Lexi announced as they pulled into the parking lot. "There's his car. Isn't it great?" She pointed to the '49 Ford Coupe.

"Is he an antique car buff?"

"Yes. He restored it himself."

"It's a real beauty. I'm impressed." Ashleigh peeked at Lexi from the corner of her eye. "Todd's cute, too. I like him."

"You hardly got to talk to him," Lexi said.

"I know, but I can tell."

"Don't judge my friends by the first meeting. Please . . ." Lexi began.

"It's okay, Lexi, really."

Lexi wasn't quite sure what Ashleigh meant, but she felt in the pit of her stomach that things weren't okay at all.

The gang had already claimed a big table at the back of the cafe. Jerry Randall nodded as Lexi and Ashleigh walked by. He was taking orders and didn't have time to talk. Binky stood up and waved them over.

"Do we have enough chairs?" Lexi asked. "Tim Anders is coming, too."

"Oh, good. It will be fun to have Tim join us."

"That's right. Tim is a nice guy."

Lexi looked from Binky to Peggy and back again. Why were they talking in that odd, stilted manner? Of course Tim was a nice guy and it would be fine if he joined them! Couldn't they think of anything more intelligent to say?

The girls took turns staring at Ashleigh. "Pretty earrings," Jennifer commented, after an uncomfortable moment of silence. "Where did you get them?"

"I made them." Ashleigh slipped an earring off and handed it to Jennifer. "It's made of porcupine quills and feathers."

Jennifer looked more closely at the earring. "Really? Is that what porcupine quills look like?"

Ashleigh was explaining how she'd made the earring when several Hi-Fives sauntered past the table making a general commotion and drawing attention to themselves.

Minda stopped in front of the table and pointed at Ashleigh. "There she is, the one I was telling you about."

Why was nothing going as Lexi'd hoped it would tonight? She wished she could start the evening over. Instead, she was forced to introduce Ashleigh to the Hi-Fives.

Minda, to her credit, was more friendly to Ashleigh than either Binky or Jennifer had been.

"I love your hair," Minda blurted. "I like that thing in it."

"It's just a little strip of rawhide with some beadwork. I did it myself."

"Really?" Minda fingered her own blonde hair. "Do you think you could teach me how? I'd like to have one of those."

"Sure," Ashleigh said. "If I can find the materials, I'd be happy to help you."

Tressa Williams, who was even more blunt and forthright than Minda, stared at Lexi's friend until Ashleigh noticed the intense scrutiny. She smiled sweetly at Tressa. "Did you have a question?"

Tressa, a master at putting her foot in her mouth, blurted, "Does your family own a tepee?"

Binky groaned and slid halfway under the table. "Tressa, please!"

Ashleigh, however, did not seem offended. Instead, she treated the question with respect. "Actually, we *do* have a tepee."

"You do?" Binky gasped and popped up from beneath the table.

"We don't live in it, of course." Ashleigh laughed at the dumbfounded expression on Binky's face. "Once in a while my dad decides to go to a pow-wow. We bring the tepee along to sleep in. My mother prefers a hotel with a shower to a campsite, but she agrees to stay in the tepee to keep my dad happy."

"Neat," Minda said.

Ashleigh obviously charmed the Hi-Fives. Gina and Tressa were laughing with her. Minda was still asking questions. What a strange turnaround!

At that moment, Tim Anders burst into the Hamburger Shack and made a beeline for Ashleigh.

"Hi, Tim. I'm so glad you came," she greeted him. Tim grinned and pulled up a chair.

Jennifer's eyebrows arched in surprise. The expressions on Binky's and Egg's faces told Lexi that they, too, were startled by the obvious warmth between Ashleigh and Tim.

"Sorry it took so long for me to get here," Tim said. "The janitor wanted me to help him push the bleachers into place so he could clean under them. It only took a few minutes, but it seemed like forever because I was in a hurry."

Ashleigh gave Tim another of her high-wattage smiles and Tim responded in kind. It occurred to Lexi that Tim Anders was an attractive boy when he smiled. He'd always been nice, pleasant, and quiet. Now, animated and eager to impress Ashleigh, Tim was . . . cute!

Tim looked worriedly at his watch. "I can't stay long. I've got my dog in the car, and she's not very patient. I'm afraid if I stay too long she'll start to chew on the seat covers."

"A dog? What kind?"

"A Dalmatian," Tim said proudly. "Her name is Fireball."

"Fireball. I don't think I've ever seen a real Dalmatian," Ashleigh said. "Except in cartoons, of course."

"Would you like to see her?" Tim asked. "She'd like a little company in the car. It might save the seat cushions."

"Could I? I love animals. Dogs are my absolute favorite." Ashleigh looked to Lexi for permission.

Lexi laughed. "Go ahead. I've seen Fireball. She's a great dog."

"Fireball isn't the only one though," Tim added. "We have new puppies at home."

Lexi could see Ashleigh visibly melting at the idea of puppies.

"Puppies? Really? Baby Dalmatians. How sweet."

"Would you like to see them?" Tim suggested eagerly. "I could drive you to my house. They're really cute."

"What do you think, Lexi?"

Lexi knew how much Ashleigh loved pets. She'd even been willing to help Lexi clean out cages at Dr. Leighton's veterinary clinic. Not many of her friends had loved animals quite *that* much.

"Go with Tim to see the puppies," Lexi suggested. "I don't mind. Besides, it's awfully noisy in here. It's hard to talk. I'll meet you at home in an hour. Tim knows where I live."

"Are you *sure* it's all right? I don't want to leave you behind or anything."

"I can see the puppies anytime. You've only got a few days. Go ahead."

"You do know how much I love animals."

"Absolutely. Scram. You're wasting time."

As Ashleigh and Tim walked off together, Lexi breathed a sigh of relief. She was happier having Ashleigh with Tim than staying here with her weird-acting friends.

After Minda and the Hi-Fives wandered off, it was quiet at the table, as though everyone were afraid to speak.

Binky broke the silence. "Why didn't you tell us Ashleigh was an Indian?" Her tone was indignant.

"Why? Would that have made a difference?"

Binky shifted uncomfortably in her chair. Peggy and Jennifer did the same.

"Maybe. It was a big surprise to me. I thought I knew everything about her. Obviously I didn't. I was a little . . . uncomfortable." Binky sounded hurt. "You could have told us!"

"Why would Ashleigh's being a Native American make you uncomfortable?"

"I just didn't know what to say to her."

"You say the same kinds of things that you'd say to anyone else, silly! Tim Anders and Minda Hannaford didn't have any trouble talking to Ashleigh. Tim wasn't uncomfortable. In fact, he seemed to like Ashleigh—a lot."

Lexi could feel outrage building within her. "Besides, it wouldn't have occurred to me to tell you that Ashleigh is Indian because I never think about it. If she'd been Irish would you have had trouble thinking of things to say to her?"

"Well . . . no . . ."

"I don't know which part of the world your grandparents came from. Or Jennifer's. Or Matt's. Does it really affect what kind of a person you are today?"

"But that's different," Binky blurted. "Our grandparents and great-grandparents, well, that was a long time ago. Ashleigh is an Indian—now!"

"I thought Indians lived on reservations or something. Is Grover's Point on a reservation?"

"No, it's not."

"Then why does she live there? Why doesn't she stay with . . . her kind?"

Lexi was stunned. She felt as though she'd been hit in the stomach.

"That sounds pretty harsh, Binky," Todd said, a warning note in his voice. "This is a free country. People have a right to live anywhere they choose."

"But what are reservations for then?" Egg saw the look on Lexi's face and held up a hand. "I don't mean to be rude about your friend, Lexi. I really don't understand."

"Ashleigh and her parents live in Grover's Point because Mr. White Eagle is a teacher at the school. He does consulting work as well. That's why he's in Cedar River now—to work at the college." Lexi glared at her friends.

"You can't blame us for not knowing much about Native Americans, Lexi."

"Egg's right. You're acting as though you're angry with us," Binky complained. "I can't help it that I'm uncomfortable, or that I don't know what to say to a person who's an Indian."

"You don't say anything special, Binky. Just act natural. Ashleigh is no different than you or I."

"She doesn't look like us."

Todd cleared his throat. "Binky, you and Egg are brother and sister. You two don't look alike. Looks don't mean anything."

Binky's shoulders sagged. "Well, I suppose that's true. It's just that she looks so . . ." Binky searched for the correct word. ". . . she's so pretty and dramatic. It doesn't feel like she belongs here. Besides, we wouldn't have been so surprised if you'd warned us, Lexi."

"You mean no one belongs in Cedar River who isn't ordinary-looking and a little bit dull?"

"That's not what I meant."

"Well, that's what you said." Lexi grabbed Binky's hands and held them tightly. "Binky, Ashleigh is a wonderful person. Just like you are. She's one of my dearest friends in the whole world. That's because of what's under her skin, not the color of it. If you don't let yourself relax and get to know her, you're going to miss a great chance to make a new friend. Just because Ashleigh's ancestors spoke Lakota instead of German doesn't mean you can't be her friend. Look at it this way. She's interesting, and I like her."

"I know, but I just feel a little funny." Binky looked at Jennifer and Peggy. "You felt it too, didn't you?"

Peggy hung her head and Jennifer looked away. "You could have warned us, Lexi. We were surprised, that's all. How would you feel if you thought we'd told you *everything* about a person and then realized we'd left out something so . . . obvious?"

Lexi was beginning to understand. Her friends were not so much prejudiced as they were surprised. They'd felt left out, betrayed. Lexi felt a surge of relief. Now that she knew where her friends were coming from, she knew they'd turn around.

"She has a different heritage, that's all. Mr. Raddis talks all the time in history class about America being a melting pot for people from every country and every race. That's what makes America special. After all, Binky, if you and Egg were to trace your ancestors back a few generations, you wouldn't find them here in America, would you? Only Ashleigh can do that."

"I don't know very much about our ancestors, do you, Egg?"

"We could ask our grandparents about it," Egg suggested.

"I feel dumb, Lexi," Binky admitted. "I guess I should know about my own heritage before I start criticizing someone else's."

Jerry Randall came to the table to take their orders and the subject was changed. After they had eaten, Lexi said good-night, then rose to go home.

"Do you want to ride with me?" Todd began. Then he grinned. "Oh, I forgot, you drove yourself tonight." He got up from his chair. "The least I can do is walk you to your car."

When they were alone, Todd put his arm around Lexi's shoulders and gave her a hug. "Don't let Binky, Egg, and the rest of them upset you, Lexi. Tonight they ran into something they didn't understand. They'd all heard you talk so much about Ashleigh that they had a picture of her built up in their minds. When they met her, they couldn't make the pictures they had in their heads jive with the real thing. They probably blamed her heritage for that, but it's not Ashleigh's problem, it's theirs."

"Thanks for understanding, Todd. I knew I could count on you." Lexi gave a weary sigh. "Of course, I thought I could count on them too. I never dreamed for a minute that any of my friends would have trouble accepting Ashleigh. Maybe she shouldn't have come here. Maybe her presence here is going to cause trouble!"

Chapter Five

"I should have pulled the shades last night when we went to bed," Lexi muttered as the sun streamed into her bedroom and across the bed. "But it was too late and I forgot about it."

"That's all right." Ashleigh stretched like a big cat on her side of the bed. "This is exactly what I'd hoped we'd do when I came to Cedar River—fall asleep talking and wake up talking. There's so much to catch up on."

Ashleigh's dark hair spread across the white pillowcase like a black wave. Her eyes were dancing prettily. She didn't look like she'd just awakened.

Lexi flopped onto her stomach and propped her chin in her hands to stare at her friend. "Okay. Tell me again about your evening with Tim."

"It was great. I like him a lot. He took me for a drive in his car and he showed me a little bit of Cedar River. I wanted him to show me more, but he refused. He said you'd be mad at him if he took away all your fun."

"He's right about that. I do want to be the first to show you Cedar River."

"Then we went to his house. He showed me the puppies. Oh, Lexi, they're so sweet. Did you know that Dalmatians are born white? The spots come later."

"Really?"

"They're the most precious little things. Tim let them out of their pen and they came running to me. They jumped and nipped and yipped and barked. I picked one up and he kept licking the underside of my chin until I thought I was going to die laughing. We played with them for a little while before Tim put them back into their pen. I think poor Fireball was getting nervous. She was happy to have her puppies back beside her."

"Then what?" Lexi wiggled her toes over the edge of the bed.

"Tim made us root beer floats. Big ones with lots of ice cream. We were going to watch TV, but there was a video of old family movies in the VCR, so we watched those instead. What a kick it was seeing Tim as a little boy!" Ashleigh smiled secretively as if she'd had a thought she didn't want to share.

"And you think he's cute, right?" Lexi commented.

"Are you reading my mind?"

"I've had years of practice."

"I had a nice time. Tim is a great guy."

"I agree with you. When you need help with something, you can always count on Tim. He's always polite and friendly, never rude. Just an all around good guy, I guess," Lexi concluded.

"I have something to talk to you about, Lexi." Ashleigh's expression showed concerned.

"Is something wrong?"

"No, everything's all right. It's just that . . . well . . . I don't want to offend you or anything . . ."

"How could you offend me?"

"Tim asked me out for tonight too. He said he'd like to get to know me better. He invited me to a place called The Station for dinner. I told him I wasn't sure. After all, you are the one I've come to visit. I thought you might be disappointed."

Lexi whistled low and long. "The Station! Elegant! Tim must *really* like you."

"He didn't tell me it was a fancy place," Ashleigh admitted. "Tim said his dad promised he could take a date to The Station as a reward for cleaning out the garage and washing the car this past weekend. I was flattered that he asked me, but I won't go, Lexi—not if you'll be upset."

"Don't be in such a hurry to say no to Tim!" Lexi exclaimed. "I think it's great that you've made a friend in Cedar River. Tim is sweet, and obviously crazy about you. There's no nicer place to eat in Cedar River than The Station." Lexi gave Ashleigh a big hug. "Don't worry about me. It's neat that you have a date. You'll be able to go home to Grover's Point and tell everyone how much fun you had."

Ashleigh laughed and threw her arms around Lexi. "It's no wonder I've missed you so much. You're so understanding. I have to admit I really would like to go out with Tim."

"You'd be crazy not to!" Lexi was happy that Ashleigh had made a friend and would be occupied this evening.

Though she didn't say it, Lexi preferred that Ashleigh not spend time with her friends after the way they'd been behaving. She still had a bad feeling about last night. Binky, Egg, Jennifer, and Peggy were poor at hiding their feelings. Whatever they felt or thought was always clearly written across their features. She didn't want Ashleigh to sense any of their discomfort.

"I've got an idea!" she said with a sudden burst of energy. "Let's pick out an outfit for you to wear tonight."

Ashleigh frowned. "I didn't bring many things. How nice did you say The Station was?"

"Fancy. Let me look in your suitcase. If there's nothing suitable, we can find something in my closet."

"I brought a skirt to wear for church," Ashleigh said. "It's nothing special."

Lexi studied the garment Ashleigh was holding. "It's nice, but not quite dressy enough. Come on." She opened her own closet door.

"I thought you didn't sew much anymore!" Ashleigh commented. Lexi's closet was lined with clothes.

"I should start sewing for other people. That way I wouldn't wind up with so many clothes for myself." Lexi pawed through her dresses and pulled out a brown shirtwaist with a short narrow skirt and long sleeves. "Here, this will do it."

"That's too cute, Lexi. I can't borrow that."

"Sure you can. Brown isn't my color anyway. It will be spectacular with some of those beautiful earrings you make. Your legs are a little longer than mine. I hope it's not too short. Try it on."

Reluctantly, Ashleigh slipped the dress over her head. "I can't. I'd be taking one of your special dresses, Lexi. I love this."

"Good. It looks absolutely fabulous on you."

The two girls stared at Ashleigh's reflection in

the mirror. "It does everything for you that it doesn't do for me," Lexi assured her friend. "Let's find shoes to go with it."

When they'd found some to match, Lexi worked with Ashleigh's long black hair.

"I wish I could get some curl to stay in it," Ashleigh said regretfully as Lexi pulled her hair into a dramatic ponytail. "But it just slides right out because it's so thick and heavy."

"It feels like silk to me. Why don't you wear it back with a headband? Just before you go, I'll put some curl on the ends with the curling iron."

Ashleigh turned to face her friend. "Are you *sure* you don't mind that I'm going out for dinner tonight? I feel so guilty! I came to visit you and here I am, running off."

"You came to have a good time and to get to know my friends. Tim is one of my friends. You'll have a good time. Therefore, you'll be doing exactly what you came to do! I'm really happy for you. I want to hear all about it when you come home."

"You're great, Lexi. Thanks again."

Lexi changed the subject. She didn't want Ashleigh to worry about this evening, and Lexi needed the time to get her own head together anyway. "Let's go downstairs and have breakfast. It's after ten-thirty."

The two girls padded barefoot toward the kitchen. They stopped in the dining room just short of the kitchen door. The sound of men's voices drifted through the closed door from the other room.

"Who's that?" Ashleigh whispered.

"One of them is my dad," Lexi said. She leaned a little closer. The men were talking loudly.

"The other sounds like Tim Anders' father," Ashleigh said. "I met him last night. He came home as Tim and I were leaving. He wasn't very friendly."

"I wonder what he's doing here." Lexi pointed to the dining room table. "Mom left juice and rolls for us. We can eat in here. That way, we won't interrupt Dad and Mr. Anders."

"They sound excited," Ashleigh commented. "They must be discussing something important."

Ashleigh and Lexi sat down at the table and Lexi poured orange juice into two tall glasses. As she passed Ashleigh the rolls, she realized they were unwittingly listening to a conversation that they were not supposed to hear.

"You've got to calm down, Anders." Dr. Leighton's voice was soothing. "You're pacing around the kitchen like a caged tiger."

"I can't calm down. I'm too upset. It's all because of that girl Tim brought to the house last night."

"That 'girl' is Ashleigh White Eagle. She's one of my daughter's best friends."

"That's fine for you, Leighton. If you want your daughter to be her friend, I don't mind. I can't tell you what to do. If you want her in your house, you can have her. But I *do* have the right to say what happens in my own home. My son Timothy hasn't dated much. He's an innocent, inexperienced young man. It's my duty as a parent to protect him."

"Protect him from what? You're not making any sense, Anders!"

"I said *protect* and I mean *protect*. Tim is crazy about that girl he brought home last night!"

"That's rather hard to believe considering that Ashleigh only arrived yesterday."

"Don't you remember how it was for you when you were young, Jim? A beautiful girl, a little flattery . . . why, that's probably all it took to make you fall head-over-heels in love."

"I hope I had more common sense, Anders. Tim has common sense, too. He's a good kid. The kids looked at a litter of puppies. That seems harmless to me."

"Harmless? Huh! It's apparent to me that Tim has fallen for this girl. He's asked her out again tonight. He wants to take her to The Station for dinner."

"Where does a boy Tim's age get money to go to The Station for dinner?" Lexi heard her father ask.

"I'd told him he could take a friend there," Mr. Anders admitted. "Tim worked hard cleaning my garage and washing the car last weekend. But I never imagined he'd take someone like this."

"Someone like this—meaning an attractive, charming friend of Lexi's?"

"Don't be so naive, Leighton. You understand perfectly well why I have to nip this relationship in the bud."

"No, I don't understand at all," Dr. Leighton said stubbornly.

"Because she's an Indian, of course!"

"Is that what this is all about?"

"Tim's vulnerable right now. He needs guidance, leadership . . . standards."

"Tim does have standards." Dr. Leighton defended the boy who was not there to defend himself. "And honestly, I don't see what all the fuss is about."

Lexi could hear Mr. Anders pacing the floor.

"Frankly, Leighton, I don't want my son dating

outside his race. Tim is too young to handle it."

There was a deadly silence on the other side of the kitchen door. Lexi instinctively knew her father was angry, but when he spoke, his voice was still calm.

"I don't think that taking a friend to dinner is something that needs to be *handled*. Tim didn't ask this girl to marry him. He asked her to go out to dinner."

"But of all the people he could have asked, did it have to be her?" It was obvious from his tone that Mr. Anders had some very negative ideas about Native Americans. "I don't want my son to marry outside his race. Therefore, he'd better learn right now . . . early . . . before he gets hurt, that he might as well not even date non-Caucasians.

"You can stop the kids from going out tonight, Dr. Leighton. I've talked to Tim and he's furious. But that girl is staying here with you. You'll have to put your foot down."

"I just don't understand you, Anders. I can't comprehend—"

"Tim and Ashleigh can be friends if they want to," Anders conceded, "but they can't date. I won't have it."

Lexi glanced across the table at Ashleigh. She was frozen in her chair, a tortured expression on her face. A little cry of anguish slipped from her lips as she pushed away from the table.

Before Lexi could catch her, Ashleigh disappeared up the stairs.

Lexi could hear deep, gut-wrenching sobs from her bedroom above the dining room. She heard Mr. Anders' voice as he departed.

"I'm disappointed in you, Leighton. I thought you'd have a clearer head about this. You talk a believable line about being a good father, but when things get tough, you're not willing to jump in and actually be one."

The back door slammed. Lexi jumped from her seat and ran into the kitchen where her father stood with a dismayed expression on his face.

"Daddy," Lexi's voice broke and tears came to her eyes.

"You didn't overhear that, did you, Lexi?"

"All of it. We were having breakfast in the dining room."

Dr. Leighton's shoulders sagged. "Oh, no. How terrible. Ashleigh too?"

Lexi nodded woodenly. "She's upstairs crying her heart out right now."

"I should have taken him outside. I didn't hear you come downstairs. I thought we were alone."

"We were barefoot," Lexi admitted. "I never expected to hear . . . that."

"No one ever does." Dr. Leighton eyes flashed with anger. "In many ways, Mr. Anders is a fine man, but this is a side of him that I've never seen before. I didn't expect it for even a moment."

"I don't understand, Dad. I just don't understand."

Dr. Leighton took Lexi's hand and led her to the kitchen table. "Sit down, honey. We have things to discuss."

"He sounded as though he *hated* Ashleigh. He doesn't even know her! He only saw her for a few moments last night. How can he hate her when he doesn't even *know* her?"

"You know what the word *prejudice* means. Mr. Anders has pre-judged Ashleigh."

"Just because she's Indian?"

"I'm afraid so. Anders doesn't want his son having anything to do with her."

"That's weird!"

"In your mind it is, but not in his. There are many people in this country who are prejudiced. At some time in their lives, they were taught that there was something wrong with people of races, cultures, or heritages other than their own. That idea, that prejudice, is deeply embedded in their thoughts. Apparently, Mr. Anders is one of those people. When he saw a Native American come into his home, all the fears and misconceptions that he's learned in his life came forward and frightened him."

"So because Mr. Anders is prejudiced about Indians, Tim can't take Ashleigh out for supper? That's not fair! Besides, it doesn't make sense. God made all of us. What's the difference between us, really, if we've all got the same Creator?"

"I'm glad you're able to think that way, Lexi. I'm deeply sorry that Tim's father can't." Dr. Leighton looked upward in the direction of Lexi's bedroom. "I'd better talk to Ashleigh," he said. "Although I'm not sure what I can say to comfort her."

Lexi and Dr. Leighton ascended the stairs to the second floor. Lexi could still hear Ashleigh sobbing in the bedroom.

"Ashleigh, can we come in?" Lexi murmured.

"No. I want to be alone."

Lexi looked at her father. He shook his head. "That's not a good idea right now."

"Ashleigh, Dad and I are coming in. We need to

talk to you." When they entered the room, Ashleigh sat up, hastily rubbing away the tears. It was no use. Her eyes were red and swollen and her lips trembled.

"Ashleigh, I have to apologize," Dr. Leighton began. "I would never have invited Mr. Anders into this house if I'd realized his purpose in coming."

"It's not your fault, sir." Ashleigh turned anguished eyes toward Dr. Leighton. "But I can't understand why anyone would hate me because of my race. That doesn't make me evil, does it?"

"Hardly, Ashleigh. Don't even think that way."

"Mr. Anders talked as though I were. He sounded as if I were going to *hurt* Tim by going to dinner with him, by being his friend."

"Mr. Anders was wrong, Ashleigh. You must understand that. What he said was inexcusable."

"But those are his honest feelings," Ashleigh pointed out. "My dad says everyone has a right to their own opinions."

"Although I can't argue with that, Ashleigh, Mr. Anders' opinions spring from some very misguided beliefs."

Ashleigh seemed to be settling down, Lexi noted. Her father had that effect on people. Just as he was able to sooth a frightened pet, he could comfort someone who was upset or in pain.

Ashleigh scrubbed at her eyes again, trying to banish the tears. "I just don't get it. I don't get it all." She looked up at Dr. Leighton. "What is Mr. Anders so afraid of?"

"I can't excuse Mr. Anders for what he said or did, but I can try to explain where he's coming from.

"You hit the nail on the head when you asked what Mr. Anders is afraid of. His fear was speaking for him today, not his common sense, intelligence, or kindness . . . only his fear."

"Fear of Ashleigh?" Lexi asked, staring at the slender girl sitting on her bed, so hurt and vulnerable.

"Not exactly. He's afraid of people who are different from himself. That includes Ashleigh and hundreds of others. Mr. Anders is afraid of the cultural and racial differences between people. He believes that the kind of persons his ancestors were and he is, are the best. He's not willing to look at other heritages, cultures, and races and discover what's good about them. This lack of knowledge often leads to unfounded prejudices and stereotypes."

"What's so scary about me?" Ashleigh demanded. She stood up and looked at herself in the mirror. "Do I look mean or cruel, like I might hurt Tim? I didn't have a single idea in my head other than having fun and making a new friend. What's so horrible about that?"

"How could Ashleigh hurt Tim?" Lexi asked. "What would be so bad about them being a couple?"

Dr. Leighton sighed deeply. "This is a tough issue."

"I hope you can explain it! I certainly can't," Ashleigh said bitterly.

"I believe that Mr. Anders fears for his son's future."

"I'm only staying a couple days," Ashleigh protested.

"Mr. Anders sees you and Tim as a couple with vast cultural differences. By separating you now, at your age, Anders thinks he's protecting Tim from future hurts and from other people's prejudices."

"He thinks that I'm not good enough for Tim?"

"Mr. Anders isn't thinking clearly about anything at all right now. It's obvious that he doesn't know many Native Americans or he'd know what fine people they are."

"That's Mr. Anders' big error," Lexi said. "His mistake is not getting to know the *person* that Ashleigh is. He's lumping all Native Americans into one pile."

"He should realize that not all Indians are alike anymore than all Norwegians are alike or all Americans are alike," Ashleigh said.

"That's one way to fight prejudice, Ashleigh," Dr. Leighton said. "People must grow to be friends, one on one. Slowly they will begin to understand that the color of a person's skin or the continent on which his ancestors were born has nothing to do with the value of the person."

"It's what's inside that counts. My mom and dad are always saying that. I think it's insulting that he thinks that every Indian is alike, or that because I have dark skin and hair I might be bad for his son."

"It seems to me," Lexi added, "we need to study more about Native Americans."

"You can say that again," Ashleigh said. "People assume that just because I'm a Sioux Indian that I know all about the Chippewa or the Cherokee. I've even had people ask me if my grandfather knew Chief Joseph!"

Lexi swallowed uncomfortably. "Who's that?"

Ashleigh burst out laughing. "Chief Joseph was a Nez Perce Indian."

Lexi blushed a deep red. "I guess I'm as dumb as the next guy."

"But at least you're willing to learn without passing judgment first."

Lexi nodded, not knowing what else to say.

"What can I do about this, Dr. Leighton?" Ashleigh asked. "I don't know how to make Mr. Anders reject the stereotypes he's had all his life. I don't know how to stop his fear. Doesn't the Bible say that God made man in His own image?"

"This is Mr. Anders' problem, Ashleigh," Dr. Leighton said again. "It's a decision he'll have to make on his own."

Ashleigh began to pace back and forth in the room. "Even though this is the first time this has happened to me, I have a feeling it's not going to be the last. I've been lucky so far, living in Grover's Point where everyone's known and accepted me all my life. Maybe once I leave Grover's Point, I'll find all sorts of people who don't like me just because I'm Native American."

"You can't live your life worrying about the next prejudiced person who might come along," Dr. Leighton said. "All you can do is be the very best person you know how to be. Then you can help put prejudices and fears to rest."

"I want to be judged for myself. I don't want other people to think they know who I am just because I'm an Indian."

"That's the spirit!" Lexi said enthusiastically, happy to hear some of Ashleigh's old spit and fire coming back.

"Thanks to you two, I'm feeling a lot better now." Ashleigh glanced ruefully at the outfit she and Lexi had laid out on the bed, the one she'd planned to wear to dinner with Tim.

"I wonder how Tim feels about this?"

"This isn't Tim's doing, Ashleigh. This is his father's," Lexi reminded her.

"I know. I hope he doesn't think I don't want to go out with him anymore. I'd *still* go if it weren't for his father." Ashleigh lifted her chin and squared her shoulders. "If I have to prove myself to Mr. Anders and everyone else who doesn't like or trust Indians, then I guess that's how it will be. I have to be the nicest and the best person that I can. Maybe someone, by meeting me, will begin to be less prejudiced. I'm not ashamed of who I am. After all, God made me."

Lexi moved to the bed and threw her arms around Ashleigh. "You bet He did. And God doesn't make mistakes."

Chapter Six

Benjamin pounded loudly on Lexi's bedroom door. "Are you guys in there?"

"Yes, Benjamin. Please wait."

"Are you getting ready for church?"

"We're trying, Ben."

"Mom says breakfast is ready and it's almost time to go."

Lexi heard her little brother's footsteps recede down the hall as she slipped a skirt on and zipped it up.

"There. How do I look?"

"Why did I ever let you talk me into this?" Ashleigh moaned. She was combing her hair and looked very pretty in the skirt and blouse she'd picked for the occasion. "I should have said no the very first time you asked me. Look at this." Ashleigh held out her trembling fingers.

There was another knock at the bedroom door. "Girls, I want you to eat before we leave."

Ashleigh opened the door and walked into the hallway. "I am so nervous, I think I'm going to throw up," she declared. "I can't believe I said I'd do this."

Lexi and her mother exchanged a smile. Mrs. Leighton put her arm around Ashleigh's shoulders.

"There's no need to be nervous, Ashleigh. I think it's wonderful that you and Lexi are going to sing during our church service."

"I think I'll faint."

Lexi smirked. "She gets this way before she sings, Mom. I've seen it happen a dozen times."

"Then why are you putting me through it again?" Ashleigh groaned.

"Because I've missed singing with you. As soon as you get up in front of all those people, your nervousness will vanish. You'll sing like a bird."

"Yeah, right. A crow."

Lexi ignored her friend. "I always feel like I'm a real star when I sing with you. You have such an incredible voice. You make anyone who sings with you sound great."

"Flattery will get you nowhere," Ashleigh warned. "I'm a nervous wreck. I'm going to be performing before a congregation of complete strangers."

In an attempt to calm her nerves, Mrs. Leighton asked, "Have you been taking voice lessons, Ashleigh?"

"Yes. I'm still taking from Mrs. Latimer." Ashleigh smiled. "She's really good for my ego. She feels I'm good enough to go professional. Can you believe it?"

"I can," Lexi enthused. "There aren't many voices as beautiful as yours."

"What do your parents think?" Mrs. Leighton asked.

"They aren't encouraging me to go professional. They feel it's important that I be a normal teenager. There's time enough for that later."

"Seems sensible to me," Mrs. Leighton agreed. "It's not easy to be a musician with the traveling and the pressures involved. I'd enjoy my high school and college years first if I were you."

"That's exactly what my parents have said."

"If your vocal teacher thinks you're good enough to go professional, then we're especially lucky to have you singing in church today. My friends will be surprised." *And* Lexi added to herself, *so will anyone else who thinks the only kind of music Indians make is with tom-toms and war drums!*

After the episode with Mr. Anders, Lexi was more determined than ever to make her own friends understand how wrong it was to make judgments about people based on the color of their skin.

————

"There you are. I've been waiting for you." Todd stood on the front steps of the church with a smile lighting his features.

"Why haven't you already gone down to Sunday school?"

"The teacher wants to use a filmstrip. They're still setting up," Todd explained. "Are you coming too, Ashleigh?"

"I wouldn't miss it." Ashleigh's smile was bright and wide. Only Lexi knew that it was forced, and how broken Ashleigh felt inside.

A large group had gathered in the basement of the church. Egg waved them over to chairs he and Binky had saved.

"I thought you two would never come," Binky gasped. "I had to tell four people these places were taken. Hurry up! Sit down." Lexi was surprised at their changed attitudes.

Egg and Binky had something on their minds and, as usual, were eager to share it. "I have something to say to you, Ashleigh," Binky blurted. Her face and the tips of her ears turned pink. "Egg and I went to the library yesterday morning."

"Oh?" Ashleigh said hesitantly, obviously wondering what that might have to do with her.

"I wasn't going to tell you this, but I decided I just couldn't keep it to myself. We checked out some books on the history of the Sioux Indians."

Both Lexi and Ashleigh grew tense and wary. "Egg and I spent all day yesterday reading."

"So that's where you were," Todd commented. "I wondered why you didn't stop by the garage while I was working."

"It's fascinating, Todd." Binky's eyes were shining with the delight of her new knowledge. "I learned so much new stuff that I can hardly believe it.

"Was I ever dumb!" she admitted. "I thought I knew everything about Indians because I knew they lived in tepees and hunted buffalo. And that's about all I knew! I'm much smarter now. You're really lucky, Ashleigh."

"I am?"

Binky nodded enthusiastically. "Think of all the interesting papers you can write for school about your heritage! I'm stuck doing dumb things like 'What I Did on My Summer Vacation.'"

"Binky, you're funny," Ashleigh laughed. "I appreciate that you went to all that effort to learn and understand something you didn't know about before. Thank you."

"Well, I learned new stuff, too," Egg added indignantly.

Ashleigh grew more relaxed. Lexi gave a little prayer of thanks for her friends, who, though not perfect, tried so hard to be genuine and sincere.

"Shhh," Todd whispered. "Looks like the filmstrip's ready." Ashleigh and Lexi turned their attention to the front of the room. It wasn't until the end of the hour that Lexi glanced around again. Attendance was good. Only one person was absent from class . . . Tim Anders. Did his father have him skip Sunday school just to avoid Ashleigh?

After class, everyone went to the foyer of the church to meet their parents for the service. Ben was already there waving a picture he'd colored in class.

"See this?" He thrust the paper in front of Lexi's face.

"Pretty, Ben. Flowers."

"Lilies of the field." He pointed to some blue and brown specks at the top of the paper. "And these are the birds of the air. Do you know what verses we studied today?"

"I have a pretty good idea, Ben." Lexi began to quote: "Why do you worry about clothes? Look at the flowers in the field. See how they grow . . ."

"Ahhh, you already knew my verse." Ben looked disappointed.

Lexi ruffled his hair. "That was one of my favorite verses when I was your age, Ben."

"But I was going to surprise you." Ben stuck out his lower lip.

It was Ashleigh who charmed Ben out of pouting. She took his hands in her own. "When we get home, Ben, would you draw a picture just like that for me?

I'd like to take it back to Grover's Point. I'll show it to your friends and tell them what you've learned."

Ben's eyes lit immediately. "Okay. I'll draw you two pictures—or three!"

"As many as you want. I'll take them all."

"What a sweet talker you are," Binky told Ashleigh.

"I can't help myself when there's a cutie like Ben involved."

They were all laughing over the little episode when Tim Anders arrived with his parents. Lexi could feel Ashleigh grow very still as Tim and his family entered the foyer. Tim kept his eyes lowered and would not look up as he passed.

"Hi, Tim," Egg said brightly, unaware of what had transpired at the Leighton home.

"Hi," Tim mumbled. "See you later."

"Looks like he didn't get a very good night's sleep," Egg commented after Tim was gone. "I wonder what's wrong."

Lexi could see the shame and embarrassment in Tim's posture. Her heart went out to him. Lexi shuddered to think what angry words were exchanged at the Anders' household.

She was jarred from her thoughts as Ashleigh leaned close and whispered, "Say a prayer for them, will you?" She inclined her head toward the Anders family.

The service moved quickly. Soon it was time for Lexi and Ashleigh to sing. Lexi placed the palms of her hands on her stomach to quiet the butterflies. Ashleigh held out her hand and Lexi noticed that it was quivering.

"Here we go," Lexi whispered as Pastor Lake

said, "We're very privileged to have some special music today . . ."

Lexi and Ashleigh moved toward a microphone that had been set up for them. Her own fears ebbed away as she looked across the congregation of familiar, friendly faces. "Pastor Lake asked me to introduce our song and our guest. This is my friend, Ashleigh White Eagle, from Grover's Point. We've had a wonderful time this weekend renewing a friendship that means a lot to both of us.

"When Ashleigh and I discussed what we should sing, we decided on a song that speaks of friendship, and the best friend we all have in Jesus, *What a Friend We Have in Jesus*. After that, Ashleigh's going to sing *Amazing Grace*."

Lexi looked at Ashleigh and then at the church organist who had moved to the piano to accompany them. They began to sing.

It was different today, Lexi thought. Their notes seemed to take on a life of their own and swell throughout the sanctuary. The simple old hymn was filled with new meaning for her, and Lexi could sense that others felt the same way.

When the song was over, Lexi squeezed Ashleigh's hand and dropped back, leaving her alone at the mike. As she listened to Ashleigh's solo, Lexi marveled at the way her friend's voice had matured. Lexi was so moved she almost forgot to step forward to join her for the final verse.

After they returned to their seats, Pastor Lake spoke again from the pulpit. "When Marilyn Leighton called to say that Lexi and her friend had offered to do the special music today, I was delighted. I like to see young people involved in all aspects of the church. But I had no idea how lovely their singing would be. Thank you, for the gift you've given us today. My sermon will be secondary to the messages we've already received about friendship and the grace of God."

After the service, Lexi could see her parents making their way through the crowd toward her and Ashleigh. A tall, dark-haired man was with them.

"Daddy!" Ashleigh exclaimed. "I didn't know you were going to be here today."

"Jim and Marilyn called me," Mr. White Eagle said with a grin. "I wouldn't have missed this for anything. It's been far too long since I've heard you and Lexi sing together."

"Were we all right, Daddy?"

"More than all right. You girls have a beautiful gift." Mr. White Eagle gave Ashleigh a hug.

While Ashleigh was talking to her father, Lexi watched Mr. Anders edge toward them through the crowd. He was a portly man with a ruddy complexion. Though Lexi knew he was the same age as her father, he looked fifteen or twenty years older. Mr. Anders always had a self-important air about him. Sometimes Lexi felt sorry for Tim when his father fired out brisk, impatient orders.

Now, however, Mr. Anders seemed unsure of what to do. His face was flushed and he looked as though he wanted to say something, but couldn't quite get it out.

Was he going to say more cruel, unthinking things to Ashleigh's face? *or* worse yet, to her father? Lexi's stomach did a flip-flop. She breathed a sigh of relief when, at the last moment, Mr. Anders veered off into the crowd. He grabbed Tim by the shoulder and shoved him roughly through the door.

Lexi didn't know if she should be relieved or disappointed. She had hoped and prayed that something would break the barrier between Tim's father and Ashleigh.

The entire gang arrived at the Leighton house after lunch. Egg and Binky burst in first.

"You were stupendous!" Binky announced. "You could be professional."

"She already is professional," Egg said. "It was just like listening to a tape."

"You were great," Jennifer agreed as she walked through the door with Peggy and Todd.

"I wish you lived in Cedar River so you could be one of the Emerald Tones," Todd said. "We could use a voice like yours."

Lexi smiled as she watched her friends circle around Ashleigh. They certainly had warmed up since their first meeting!

"Ashleigh, we have to apologize to you," Jennifer blurted.

Lexi looked up, startled. *What?*

"Apologize? Why?" Ashleigh was as surprised as Lexi.

"For the way we acted." Jennifer continued, "I know I was kind of snooty the first time I met you, and the rest of us were, too."

"Hey," Egg started to protest, then stopped. "Well, maybe she's right. You really weren't what we expected."

"Oh?" Ashleigh said cautiously.

"We'd heard so many stories about you and

Lexi—all the things you'd done together when you were kids in Grover's Point—that we were sure we knew *everything* about you," Peggy explained. "And then you turned out to be . . ."

" . . . a Native American?"

"It was just a surprise that Lexi would leave out something so important about a person. She told us everything else about you!"

"I should apologize for that," Lexi said to her friends. "I would have told you that Ashleigh was an Indian if I'd thought it was important. I've known Ashleigh so long and so well that I don't even think about it."

"Lexi, that's the nicest thing you've ever said to me." Ashleigh put an arm around Lexi. "It makes me feel good to think that you look past who I am on the *outside* and appreciate me for who I am on the *inside*."

"We can't choose what family we're born into or what our complexion is like or what birthmarks we may have," Binky declared. "The only thing that we can control is who we are inside."

"Exactly!" Ashleigh exclaimed.

"You'll have to admit you *are* more interesting," Binky pointed out. "You come from a heritage that none of us know very much about."

"That can be resolved," Ashleigh said matter-of-factly. "Ask me anything. I can tell you stories about my grandparents and you can tell me stories about yours."

"You wouldn't mind?" Peggy asked.

"Not a bit."

Lexi smiled as she went into the kitchen for more soft drinks. It was great to see *all* her friends laughing and sharing so freely. Lexi decided that this was what maturity was all about.

Chapter Seven

Monday morning Lexi woke before the alarm clock rang. "Ashleigh . . . Ashleigh," she whispered. "It's time to get up."

Ashleigh groaned and rolled over. "I've changed my mind. I don't want to go to school with you today. I'm going to stay home and sleep."

"Chicken," Lexi accused playfully.

From beneath the covers Ashleigh muttered, "Cluck, cluck, cluck."

Lexi shook the lump in the bed. "I want you to see my school. Besides, you haven't met all my friends. There's Ruth Nelson, Brian James, and Angela . . ."

"I've met enough of your friends. I'll just hang around the house today."

Lexi plopped onto the bed next to Ashleigh and pulled the covers away from her face. "You don't want to go because of what happened this weekend. It's because of what Tim Anders' father said, isn't it?"

Ashleigh groaned and tried to roll away, but Lexi grabbed her by the shoulder. "Talk to me."

"I don't want to see Tim today. He looked so miserable in church that I thought he'd shrivel up and die. Or *I* would. I don't like being the cause of trouble in a family."

"You aren't the cause," Lexi pointed out. "Mr. Anders is. He's the one who's mixed things up, not you."

"If only Tim and I hadn't gotten along so well!" Ashleigh exclaimed. "We had so many things in common and so much to talk about. That's what really hurt when Mr. Anders came to the house and said what he did."

"You could see as well as anyone that Tim was mortified by what his father did."

"I don't know, Lexi," Ashleigh said softly. "Kids usually learn their beliefs and value systems from their parents. Maybe Tim was fooling me all along. Maybe—"

"Don't try to second-guess him. That's not fair to Tim. Give him a chance."

"I can't do that, can I?" Ashleigh laughed bitterly. "I can't give him another chance because I won't even be able to speak to Tim again. It would be better if I stayed home today. I don't want to call any more attention to myself."

"I don't want you to go home thinking that Cedar River is some little hole in the universe that doesn't recognize different cultures, races, or nationalities. Mr. Anders does not make up the whole town of Cedar River. He's prejudiced, and it's his problem. Let's not make it ours. Besides, Mr. Anders would also probably throw a fit if Leanna Wong and Tim decided to date." Lexi took Ashleigh's hand. "Please come to school with me. I'm proud to have you as my friend. I'm as proud of your heritage as you are, Ashleigh. Remember the Bible verse about not hiding your light under a bushel basket? You've got to let who you are shine."

Ashleigh gave Lexi a resigned look as she sat up.

"You could always talk me into anything," she accused.

"Hey, it's mutual." Lexi smiled widely and pulled Ashleigh from the bed. "Get into the shower fast. Breakfast will be ready soon."

When Ashleigh returned, towel-drying her hair, Lexi had laid an outfit on the bed for her to wear.

"What's that?" Ashleigh's eyes narrowed. "There's no way you're getting me to wear that to school."

"It's what you'd planned, wasn't it?"

"Yes, but that was before . . ." Ashleigh looked askance at the dramatic western-look suede skirt and vest that Lexi had laid on the bed. "I'll look like I'm playing cowboys and Indians all by myself if I wear that. I'm going to wear jeans and a T-shirt."

"The color goes beautifully with your hair," Lexi suggested.

"I'll wear a white T-shirt."

"Aren't you going to let your light shine?"

"Lexi . . ."

"Be proud of who you are."

Ashleigh threw her hands in the air. "All right. I'll wear it since there's no way I can argue with you. But . . . " She gave Lexi a warning glance. ". . . if this is an absolutely miserable day, it's going to be *your* fault."

———

Ashleigh and Lexi met Todd at the lockers. Todd was choosing books for his morning classes.

"Are you ready for a day of school in Cedar River?" he asked Ashleigh.

"Ready as I'll ever be. I even brought a notebook.

I thought I'd take a few notes to see if we were studying the same things at Grover's Point. Besides," she added softly, "I don't want to look out of place."

Lexi was beginning to worry that she'd made a mistake insisting her friend come to school today. Ashleigh was uncharacteristically nervous and edgy. Fortunately, their first three classes went smoothly and Ashleigh began to relax. Everything might have been fine if Lexi and Ashleigh had skipped fourth hour.

Mr. Raddis was absent when they entered the classroom. Definitely a bad sign. Students were already shuffling restlessly in their desks, throwing spit balls and yelling at each other across the room.

"Where's Mr. Raddis?"

"He had to go to the office for a minute. We're supposed to sit quietly."

"Sit quietly? How do we do that?" The boys in the back row laughed loudly.

"There must be *something* to do while Raddis is gone." Rita Leonard gazed around the room.

Lexi winced inwardly. *Oh, no. Not Rita. Not now. Please!* Rita was a tall, blonde girl with hard features who liked to wear heavy makeup. She was not a favorite of Lexi's, and Lexi knew Rita felt the same way about her. Rita often referred to her as "Miss Goody Two-Shoes."

Just as Lexi had feared, Rita's gaze snagged on Ashleigh in her distinctive outfit.

"Who are you?" Rita asked bluntly.

"This is my friend, Ashleigh White Eagle," Lexi spoke for Ashleigh. "She's from Grover's Point. She's visiting today."

"Oh." Rita digested that bit of information.

Much to Lexi's dismay, their conversation had attracted attention.

"Are you an Indian?" Rita asked bluntly.

Ashleigh looked Rita squarely in the eye. "Yes, I am. I'm a Sioux Indian."

The room grew quiet.

"Can you ride a horse?"

Ashleigh's eyes widened a bit. Then she smiled. "Yes I can. My father has several of them."

"Do you ride barefoot, with no saddle on the horse?"

Ashleigh smiled and the corners of her eyes crinkled with amusement. "Actually, no. I prefer to ride English-style. I ride hunt seat in the traditional English riding habit. Jodhpurs, that sort of thing."

Her statement surprised Rita into silence. Now the entire room was focused on her conversation with Ashleigh.

"Can you shoot a bow and arrow?"

The only thing that saved Lexi from sinking straight through the floor was the fact that Rita's curiosity seemed genuine. For the moment, at least, she was not making fun.

"No, but I plan to take archery when I'm in college. I hope I have enough upper arm strength to manage it." Ashleigh's polite and honest responses seemed to satisfy Rita, and they obviously impressed the other members of the class. But Rita wasn't finished.

"Can you dance and make it rain?" Rita asked sarcastically.

"I've taken classical ballet for nine years, but I haven't noticed any corresponding changes in the weather."

Rita didn't catch the irony in Ashleigh's words.

"If you can't, what kind of an Indian are you anyway?" Rita laughed and looked around the room for approval of her not-too-funny joke.

Rita's humor fell flat. Mr. Raddis stood in the doorway, listening. He cleared his throat and twenty-five pairs of eyes turned toward the door.

"Are you quite finished, Miss Leonard?" His voice was dead calm.

"Uh, yes . . . uh, sir, Mr. Raddis," Rita stammered. A fiery blush spread across her cheeks.

"I think, Miss Leonard, that you have shown an appalling lack of knowledge about Native Americans. Would you agree with me?"

Rita had no choice but to respond, "Yes, sir."

"Because I don't want you to leave this class with such a huge and offensive gap in your knowledge, I'd like you to write a ten-page, typed, double-spaced report on the early history of our country, focusing on the Native American population. Do you think you can manage that, Miss Leonard?"

Rita's face grew redder. "Yes, sir."

"Do you think there's anything else you should say at this time, Miss Leonard?" Mr. Raddis crossed his arms over his chest and looked steadily at Rita until she dropped her eyes.

"I'm sorry if I offended you, Ashleigh. Welcome to our class," Rita mumbled sullenly.

"It's okay," Ashleigh responded with a sincere smile. "If you'd like help with that report, my dad has some great Indian history books. I could get the titles from him so you could get them out of the library. It would make your report easier."

Rita's head snapped up sharply. "Huh?"

"History books—on Indians. My dad's at the college right now. I could call him at noon if you want to get started."

For a moment Lexi actually thought that Ashleigh's peacemaking actions might have some effect on Rita. Then Rita dropped her head and muttered, "No thanks. I'll do it myself."

Ashleigh shrugged. "Whatever." Although she hadn't made a friend of Rita, she'd certainly placed all the other students in the room squarely on her side.

When the class bell rang an hour later, Rita was obviously still furious about her humiliation. The rest of the students, however, had decided that Ashleigh was not only kind and savvy, but fascinating as well. Several people asked her to eat lunch with them in the cafeteria.

As they waited in line to eat, Lexi stood back and enjoyed Ashleigh's latest triumph. The morning would have been practically perfect if Rita had accepted Ashleigh's offer of help. It worried Lexi that Rita was scowling at Ashleigh from the far end of the lunch line. Rita Leonard was not a forgiving person, and Lexi desperately wanted the rest of Ashleigh's short stay in Cedar River to be fun and free of any more problems!

Chapter Eight

Egg and Binky ran across the parking lot as Lexi and Ashleigh piled into Todd's car. "Hey, wait up!" They waved their arms and yelled.

"Do you need a ride?" Todd draped one arm over the roof of the car and the other across the top of the open door.

Egg looked indignant as he came skidding to a stop in front of Todd. "Is that all you think we want you for? Your car?"

Todd grinned. "Some days. Yes."

"Well, not today," Binky said. "We want to do something really special while Ashleigh is here. Egg and I just decided what to do."

"Binky and I have decided to make a special dinner. You're all invited. It's going to be a really super evening. Both Mom and Dad have meetings tonight, so we can have the whole place to ourselves. Doesn't that sound great?"

"You're going to cook, Egg?" Todd clarified.

"You and Binky?" Lexi added.

"Yes. Isn't it great?"

Even Ashleigh looked a little worried at the suggestion. But she smiled bravely. "That's awfully nice of you."

"Egg and I have the menu all planned."

"What is it?" Todd wanted to know.

"We're not telling you," Egg said proudly. "You're going to be surprised."

"I'll be surprised all right," Todd muttered as he dropped into the driver's seat of the car. "And probably poisoned."

"Will you come?"

Lexi and Ashleigh exchanged a glance. "Sure, why not. I'm sure Mom won't mind."

"Todd?" Egg looked his friend in the eye.

"I suppose. Should I eat first?"

"Very funny, Winston. Very funny. Come and bring your appetites. We'll see you at six."

After Egg and Binky had disappeared, Todd leaned his head against the seat of the car and groaned. "What have we gotten ourselves into now?"

"Can't they cook?" Ashleigh asked.

"Who knows what the McNaughtons can do?" Lexi said with a laugh. "Never underestimate the McNaughtons, I say."

"And never overestimate them either," Todd added.

"Look at it this way—when we're done there, we can always go to the Hamburger Shack if things don't work out."

"You two are terrible," Ashleigh said. "I think it's very sweet that they're doing this because I'm here. I'm sure the meal is going to be wonderful."

Todd and Lexi exchanged a glance and nodded simultaneously. "Right. Wonderful."

Todd had already started the car and was backing out of the parking space when Ashleigh gave a small gasp. "Oh! Wait a minute. I forgot something."

Lexi was surprised. "I didn't realize you brought anything with you to school."

"My notebook," Ashleigh said. "I'd better have it because I used it for my make-up math assignment. If I forget it here, I'll have to do my math all over again."

Todd drove near the doorway and stopped. "Hop out. You can run in and get it. Do you know which locker is Lexi's?"

"I think so." Ashleigh jumped out of the car and ran inside.

"It's locker number 35!" Lexi called after her, but Ashleigh had already disappeared into the building.

In only a few minutes she returned waving the notebook in the air. "I guess I didn't know which locker was yours after all, Lexi, but I found it on the third try."

Todd dropped the girls off at Lexi's home with the promise of returning at ten minutes to six.

When Lexi and Ashleigh walked in the door, the telephone was already ringing.

"Hello, Leighton residence, Lexi speaking."

"Lexi, are you invited to Egg and Binky's tonight?" Jennifer's voice was agitated.

"Yes. Todd too. Did they invite you?"

"Plus Peggy and Matt. They wanted to invite more, but their dining room table only holds eight. Are you going?"

"Of course."

"Do you actually dare? What if they poison us or something."

"Egg and Binky wouldn't do that."

"Not intentionally, of course. But you know how they are. You've watched Egg eat. When he gets in one of his health food kicks, he puts tofu, sprouts and little green stuff on his pizza and in his ice cream. If they do something weird like that, it will gross me out. I'll throw up. I know I will."

"Don't panic, Jennifer. Everything will be fine."

"If you say so," Jennifer said doubtfully. "I'm not even sure they can cook."

Lexi laughed as she hung up the telephone. "I never dreamed how much excitement your visit would stir up, Ashleigh. That was Jennifer. She's afraid of being poisoned by her best friends."

Ashleigh flung herself into a chair. "I'll have to admit that I didn't know what to expect, either, when I came to Cedar River. None of what I thought *might* happen happened, and everything I *didn't* think would happen did."

"Sorry about that."

"Don't apologize. I've had a great time."

"Even with Tim's father and Rita?"

Ashleigh waved a hand in the air. "Oh, them. I can't worry about that. If I were going to worry about all the shortsighted people in the world, I'd be too busy to have any fun." Ashleigh looked at her watch. "We have a little time before we have to go to Egg and Binky's. Do you think we should eat something, just in case?"

————

When they arrived at the McNaughtons, every light in the house was on. Egg met them at the door wearing a white apron and a chef's hat he'd made of tag board and white paper napkins. His already tall, lanky frame looked positively gigantic in a string bean sort of way. He waved a wooden spoon in one hand and gestured with the other. "Come in. Come in."

Binky burst out of the kitchen like a ball out of a cannon. "First he wanted to do all the grocery shopping. Then he wanted to do all the cooking. Now he wants to be the one to greet you at the door as well. What am I supposed to be doing here? I am not your slave, Egg. We planned this meal together. I'm your partner, not your helper."

"She's a little touchy tonight," Egg said casually, flicking a hand in Binky's direction.

"I don't have time for that. I must return to the kitchen. Binky, take over."

When Egg had disappeared, Binky shot a daggered look through the doorway of the kitchen. "He is so bossy tonight," she grumbled. "You'd think he was Chinese or something."

"Huh?" Ashleigh, Lexi, and Todd said in unison.

"We're cooking Chinese food. You'd think he'd invented the recipes. I try to tell him stuff, but he won't listen! He says he knows all about it; that he read about it in a book. If he makes us all sick, I want you to know it's his fault, not mine."

Ashleigh put a hand over her mouth to keep from giggling. Binky picked up the tagboard hat that Egg had made for her. "Come on," she said ungraciously as she slapped the lopsided hat onto her head. "Our chef thinks you'd be interested in seeing him do the stir-fry."

"You mean we get a demonstration, too?" Lexi asked.

"Good deal," Todd muttered under his breath. "Then we can check out what it is we'll be eating."

They followed Binky into the kitchen. Jennifer,

Peggy, and Matt were already gathered around the stove.

Egg and Binky had spent their time after school chopping up food for the stir-fry. There were bits of celery and onion all over the kitchen floor.

"Yuck. What is that?" Lexi gasped, pointing at a chicken carcass resting forlornly on the counter.

"We're going to make soup out of it tomorrow," Egg assured her. "Chicken broth with homemade noodles, I think."

"Dumplings. I like dumplings," Binky said.

"Noodles."

"Dumplings."

They glared at each other.

"Egg, don't you think you'd better watch the oil in this pan?" Matt suggested.

Egg glanced worriedly at the large wok on the stove.

"What's this?" Jennifer picked up a twisted little chunk of what looked like petrified wood.

"So that's where my ginger went," Egg said. "Binky, would you chop some of that?"

"'Binky, do this. Binky, do that," Binky muttered as she took the twisted little root out of Jennifer's hand and began to peel back the outer layer and chop the inner core into fine pieces.

"Tonight," Egg began his lecture, "we are going to serve stir-fried walnut broccoli chicken. Poultry is second only to pork in popularity in the Chinese diet."

"He really *is* going to give us a lecture," Ashleigh whispered.

"Of course." Lexi smiled. Getting used to the McNaughtons took more time than Ashleigh had

had so far. No doubt Egg had memorized a cookbook for just such an occasion.

"We've taken the tender white meat from the breast for this delicious meal we are about to prepare. Chicken livers can also be stir-fried, but—"

"Ewww, gross." Jennifer put her hand over her mouth. "We're not eating liver, are we?"

Egg gave her a dirty look. "Not tonight. I *said* not tonight."

"Oh, good."

Egg waved his wooden spoon over the counter area. "As you can see, we've cut up chicken, mushrooms, broccoli, onions, celery, and water chestnuts for this delightful meal."

"I guess we'd better like vegetables," Matt muttered.

"Once the oil is heated to the proper temperature, we will add the chicken and fry it until it begins to brown." He dropped a piece of raw chicken into the pan. It sizzled, danced, and began turning brown. "It's ready! It's ready, Binky!" Suddenly Egg lost his composure. "Now what?"

"Fry the rest of the chicken, silly. When it's done take it out and add the walnuts and veggies. I'll dish up the rice while that's cooking."

Binky struggled with a huge wad of rice that refused to be released from the bottom of the pan. Finally Todd and Matt took over and wrestled the gooey mess into a serving bowl. Jennifer and Peggy filled water glasses at the table set with plates and chopsticks. Egg vigorously stir-fried vegetables until his face was a bright pink.

"It's ready everyone!" Egg yelled. "Sit down. We've got to eat."

As everyone rushed to the table, Egg staggered into the dining room carrying the huge wok full of chicken, walnuts, and vegetables.

"It actually looks good," Todd said in amazement.

"And it smells wonderful," Matt added.

Everyone was dumbfounded, except Egg. "Of course it's good. I made it. Sit down. Let's eat." He plopped the wok in the center of the table, next to the white mountain of rice. He flung his hat into the corner of the room, pulled off his apron, and sat down. "Who prays?" he said. "Me?"

"I'd like to if you don't mind," Ashleigh offered.

Ashleigh folded her hands on her lap and bowed her head. "Dear Lord, I'd like to say thanks for these days in Cedar River. They've been some of the most . . . interesting . . . I've ever experienced. Thank you for my new friends and for my oldest and dearest one, Lexi. Thanks for this food and for the cooks that prepared it. Amen."

"Well? What are we waiting for?" Egg said. "Dive in." Everyone, even Jennifer, who was still looking a little doubtful, filled their plates. Then they all sat, hands in their laps, staring at their food.

"Where are the forks?" Matt demanded.

"There are no forks. This is a Chinese meal. You have to use chopsticks."

"What did you do? Go out in the woods and whittle these?"

Binky looked indignant. "I had to buy them with my own money at the Chinese restaurant uptown. Use them."

Even Matt didn't dare argue with that. "How?" he wondered aloud.

It was a comical sight as they all struggled with

the chopsticks, each trying to discover the best method of trapping the food long enough to get it to their mouth.

"I'm going to have to lay my face on the table and just shovel it in," Jennifer said grumpily.

Todd, who had been diligently working with the sticks, finally got a piece of chicken into his mouth. "Egg, this is great!"

Egg beamed.

"I'm sure I'd think so too if I knew how to eat with these things," Peggy said. "Our food will be cold before we get it eaten."

Egg shook his head stubbornly. "If little kids can do it, you can too."

Egg was right. It wasn't so hard to learn a new skill once they set their minds to it.

Not much talking was done until the wok full of food and the mountain of rice were diminished considerably. Lexi hardly noticed when Egg stood up and disappeared into the kitchen. He came back carrying a teapot and teacups on a tray.

"What's this?" Matt said doubtfully. "We had to eat with sticks, and now we have to drink that stuff?"

"This is Chinese tea," Egg said as he placed the tray on the table.

"Tea? No way. Not for me," Matt yelped.

"Me either," said Jennifer.

"Ewww, my mother gives me tea when I'm sick. It always makes me worse."

"Chinese meal—Chinese tea," Egg said stubbornly. "Drink."

"Hey, this isn't half bad," Matt said after a few sips. "It's kind of weak, but I could get used to it with a little sugar."

"Matt, you're drinking tea with your pinky raised in the air," Peggy pointed out. "That's so sweet."

Matt made a face at her.

"I think I'll have a little more rice." Todd reached for the spoon and the bowl of rice and attempted to lift out a spoonful. His mouth dropped open in surprise as the entire bowl of rice came out on the spoon in one large, gummy blob.

"What happened to my rice?" Binky yelped.

"Are you sure it wasn't plaster of paris?" Todd said, still holding the spoon in the air with the rice clinging firmly to it.

"It's not supposed to do that, is it?"

"What do you think it's doing in our stomachs right now if it's doing that on a spoon?"

"Put that blob of rice down, Todd. You're embarrassing me."

"Sorry, Bink. I just wanted to eat a little more. It was so good."

"Binky, don't you think it's time for dessert?" Egg reminded his sister.

Binky darted into the kitchen and came back with a dainty tray of fortune cookies. She passed them with great flair and each person chose a cookie carefully.

"We'll open them together," Egg informed the group. "Then each one of us will read the fortune we received."

Solemnly, everyone snapped their fortune cookies in half and peered inside the broken wafers.

"I didn't get one."

"Me either."

"Did the fortune fall out of my cookie?"

"Hey, mine's empty."

Only Binky didn't complain. Lexi was the first to notice her bright red cheeks and sheepish expression. "Binky? Do you have a fortune in your cookie?"

"No," Binky said softly.

Egg looked up from the far end of the table. "Binky, you were in charge of these cookies. Where are the fortunes?"

"Well . . . uh . . . ahem," Binky stammered.

"Binky McNaughton, what did you do with the fortunes in these cookies? The bag said there was a fortune in every cookie."

"I've got all your fortunes. Just don't get so huffy about it," Binky said indignantly. "I'll hand them out."

"You have all the fortunes? Why aren't they in the cookies?"

Binky rolled her eyes toward the ceiling. "It's simple, really. I wanted to make sure no one got a dumb fortune. Besides, I was curious, so I thought I'd just open one cookie and see how good the fortunes were."

"Binky . . ."

"Well, just one. I opened it and it had a pretty good fortune in it, but nothing special, so I ate the cookie. Later, I started to wonder about the other fortunes. I thought that if they were dumb, nobody would have any fun with them. That's when I decided to check them out."

"How could you do that? None of the cookies were broken," Lexi said.

"It wasn't hard. I noticed this little corner of paper sticking out of one of the cookies. I knew it was the fortune. I thought that if I just pulled on it a little bit with tweezers, the fortune would come out and I could read it and make sure it was all right."

"Binky, you didn't."

"They came out easily. I just had to tug a little bit. Every one was sticking out. Before you knew it, I had all the fortunes out of the cookies."

"You pulled all the fortunes out of the fortune cookies?"

"I was going to put them back," Binky said defiantly. "It's just that I couldn't get them back in as easily as they came out. Those dumb cookies are bent in the middle!"

"I can't believe this." Egg lowered his face into his hands.

Binky pulled a handful of white paper scraps out of her pocket. "Here are your fortunes. You're just getting your fortune and your cookie separately, that's all."

"I just can't believe you did that, Binky!" Egg screeched.

"Oh, be quiet. Just take a fortune. Does it matter whether you break the cookie open and get the fortune or just pick your fortunes separately?"

Everyone's attention was drawn to a choking sound from the far side of the table. Ashleigh was laughing so hard that tears were running down her cheeks and she was gasping for air.

"This is the funniest thing . . . I have ever seen . . . in my entire life! I love it. I just love it." She wiped the tears of laughter from her cheeks and held her sides. "Oh, my stomach hurts."

Everyone—except Egg and Binky—joined in Ashleigh's merriment.

Egg was still angry. "You can never be in charge of dessert again," he threatened.

"Who says I'd ever want to be? Besides, I could have written better fortunes than the ones we got in those cookies anyway. I should have baked my own. Then I would have known what fortune went into what cookie and I wouldn't have been curious. . . ."

Because of all the laughter and silliness, it took nearly an hour to clean up. When Lexi, Ashleigh, and Todd finally said goodbye, Ashleigh impulsively threw her arms first around Egg, then Binky. She smacked each of them with a large noisy kiss.

"I will never forget this meal. Thank you."

The McNaughtons grinned proudly. Once the door was closed, Lexi and Ashleigh heard Binky say to her brother, "I couldn't help that I was curious about the fortunes. Weren't you?"

They waited until they got to the car to burst into laughter again.

"Those two deserve a prize. They really do. I love them." Ashleigh leaned back in the seat. "I wish I could take them home to Grover's Point."

"I know why you'd want to do that," Todd said. "Because no one would believe what happened tonight. You have to experience the McNaughtons in order to believe them."

"It's going to be a real let-down to return to Grover's Point."

"Are you sure it won't be a relief?" Lexi asked.

Ashleigh shook her head. "I know how worried you've been, Lexi. Don't let the trouble with Mr. Anders and Rita Leonard get you down. I haven't. Think about all the positive things that have happened. Look at all the great people I've met! I wouldn't trade any of this—especially not the dinner tonight." Ashleigh grew pensive. "Well, perhaps there is *one* thing

I would change if I could . . ."

"What's that?"

"I would have liked it if Tim and I could have been friends." There was sadness in her voice as she spoke. "It's tough to know that you're separated from someone forever because of prejudice." Then Ashleigh squared her shoulders. "But I can't change that. That's something that people have to do for themselves." She grinned. "I'll bet I have fascinating dreams tonight."

"Why?"

"I'll either be thinking about Egg, Binky, and the fortune cookies or that rice turning to cement."

Lexi groaned. "It's going to be a long night."

The next morning, Ashleigh was eager to go to school.

"This is a switch from yesterday," Lexi commented as Ashleigh pulled a sweatshirt over her turtleneck.

"I've decided I don't want to miss another thing. Last night I got a taste of the McNaughton craziness. I want to be at school for whatever happens next."

"I know what you mean. With Binky and Egg, there's always a party . . . or an accident . . . about to happen. You just never know which."

When they reached the school, Lexi groaned. "We should have hurried this morning. We're late."

The hall was congested with students. Lexi and Ashleigh had just greeted Mrs. Waverly when a loud yell broke through the other noises in the hallway.

Rita Leonard was screeching at the top of her lungs, "It's gone! My necklace is gone. It was right here in my locker. I left it here yesterday."

Everyone in the hallway froze in their spots, watching and listening.

"Excuse me," Mrs. Waverly said as she pushed through the crowd toward Rita's side.

"My grandfather gave me that locket."

"Calm down, Rita," Mrs. Waverly said. "There's no way I can help you when you're so upset."

Rita's face was flushed and her eyes were bright. "I loved that locket."

"Where, exactly, was the locket?" Mrs. Waverly asked.

"Hanging on the inside hook in my locker. Right there." Rita pointed to the interior of her locker. "I took it off for gym class yesterday. I hung it on that little hook. I usually put it on right after class, but I didn't have time yesterday. I'd planned to put it on this morning but now it's missing."

"Are you *sure* you put it on the hook, Rita? Perhaps you forgot to take it off and wore it to class. Maybe we should look in the gym and the locker room."

"I'm absolutely positive that I took the locket off and hung it there." Rita pointed at the empty hook. "And now it's gone."

"If you had something as valuable as a necklace in your locker, Rita, why didn't you lock it? After all, you have a padlock."

"I never lock my locker. No one here does. You know that, Mrs. Waverly." Then Rita's eyes narrowed and she looked up. Lexi could feel her gaze burning toward her and Ashleigh. "We didn't have to secure our lockers—until now."

"What is that supposed to mean, Rita?" Mrs. Waverly asked quietly.

"No one in Cedar River ever locks their locker. Lots of people knew I kept my locket on that hook. No one ever touched it until now." She lifted her arm and pointed directly at Ashleigh. "The only thing that's changed around here in the last twenty-four hours is her. She's the one who stole it. The Indian did it." Rita's eyes narrowed as she spat out the ugly words, "Thief! Thief!"

Lexi stepped forward. "No way, Rita. How dare you accuse my friend . . ."

"She was snooping around by the lockers after school yesterday. I saw her opening and closing locker doors. She did it at least three times."

Lexi was about to protest when a cold chill washed over her. *Ashleigh's notebook*. She'd gone in for it after school last night. Lexi remembered what Ashleigh had said when she'd returned to the car. *She'd found my locker on the third try.*

"Ashleigh wouldn't take anything. I've known her all my life. She's not a thief."

Lexi wondered if Rita was trying to get even with Ashleigh. After all, it was because of Ashleigh that Rita had managed to embarrass herself so badly in Mr. Raddis' class. Still, the locket was gone and Ashleigh had been seen alone by the lockers—opening them.

Rita was sobbing now. "My grandparents are both dead. It was all I had from them. Give it back, you thief. Give it back!"

"But I didn't . . . I didn't . . . you have to believe me," Ashleigh stammered, her face ashen.

Mrs. Waverly laid a firm hand on Rita's shoulder. "I'm sure there is a reasonable explanation for this, Rita."

Todd moved toward the lockers. "What are you doing?" Rita said sharply.

"I'm taking a look inside your locker, Rita. You don't mind, do you?"

"It's not there. I looked."

"I didn't say it was. I just want to take a look." Todd squatted by the locker and peered inside.

From where she was standing, Lexi could see that the hook was empty. Rita's books were scattered on the floor.

Todd leaned forward and put his hand in the locker. Lexi could hear the grinding of metal as he pushed on the tin and popped it outward. When he removed his hand, he was holding something.

"Is this yours?" Dangling at the end of his finger was a heart-shaped locket on a gold chain.

Rita gasped. "Where was it? I didn't see it in there."

Todd stood up and handed Rita her locket. "It must have fallen off the hook. When you threw your books on top of it, the chain got wedged into the seam between the locker floor and the sidewall. It might be scratched or dented a little, but it was there, in the locker, where it was supposed to be."

Rita grabbed the locket to her chest, flushed and embarrassed. Ashleigh sank weakly against a wall in relief.

Lexi felt her knees shaking and she wished she had a chair nearby to collapse into.

"Go on to class, all of you," Mrs. Waverly said sharply to the crowd. "This is none of your business. Everything is settled, so please be on your way."

When the crowd dispersed, Mrs. Waverly turned

to Rita. "Rita, I think you have something to say to Miss White Eagle."

For the second time in less than twenty-four hours, Rita apologized to Ashleigh. "I'm sorry I thought you stole my locket."

Ashleigh nodded weakly.

"I was so scared," Rita stammered. "It really is the only thing I have left of my grandparents. I thought because you are, you know . . ." Her voice drifted away as she realized that anything she might say would only do more harm.

"Rita, I want to talk to you in my office after school tonight," Mrs. Waverly said firmly.

Rita looked surprised. "But I didn't do anything."

"Nevertheless, I think we need to have a little talk."

Lexi took Ashleigh by the arm and steered her down the hall. As they turned away, Lexi heard Mrs. Waverly mutter under her breath, "The student lecture this morning can't come a minute too soon for me."

Chapter Nine

"Are you all right?" Lexi asked as she and Ashleigh walked down the hall toward the first hour class.

"A little shaky, that's all."

"I can't believe she did that." Lexi was indignant. "She was just trying to get even for yesterday."

"I really think she was worried about the locket, Lexi. Besides, she *did* see me looking through lockers last night," Ashleigh pointed out. "In a way, I don't blame her."

"I wanted your visit to be so perfect and instead all these awful things have happened!" Lexi wailed.

"Great things have happened too," Ashleigh said. "Don't look at the negative, look at the positive. Every time I want a good laugh, all I have to do is remember your face when Binky said that she'd taken the fortunes out of those cookies with tweezers. I wouldn't trade that image in my mind for a million dollars."

Even though she was upset, Lexi had to smile. Ashleigh was right. The visit hadn't been a total disaster.

"I suppose you're right. Still, I wonder what Mrs. Waverly meant."

"Meant about what?"

"As we were walking away she said something about a lecture not coming a minute too soon."

Ashleigh's face fell. "Oh, that was supposed to be a surprise!"

Now Lexi was really puzzled. "What are you talking about?"

"My father's coming to school today."

"He is? Why?"

"To talk about some of the things he's been discussing in his seminar at the college. Apparently the high school administration feels they haven't done enough with Native American studies and invited him to speak today.

"I wanted it to be a surprise. Now, after all the trouble I've had, I suppose Mrs. Waverly is glad that Dad's coming to support me." Ashleigh sighed and raked her fingers through her long dark hair. "Frankly, I'm sorry he's coming."

"I think it's a great idea. I don't know nearly enough about Native Americans."

Lexi took Ashleigh by the hand. "We'd better hurry or we'll be late for our first class."

———

The first hour was almost over when a voice came over the intercom. "We'll be having a special program in the gym this morning at nine thirty-five. All students please report to the gym after the class bell. Thank you."

Lexi glanced at Ashleigh. "Nervous?"

Ashleigh nodded. "When I first found out that Dad was going to do this, I was excited. Now I'm not so sure. Dad's really sensitive about issues involving prejudice."

"That's understandable—especially where his own daughter is concerned." Lexi smiled reassuringly at her friend. "Let's go hear him."

When they filed into the gym, Mr. White Eagle was already deep in conversation with Mr. Raddis and Mrs. Waverly. He towered over them both. Lexi was struck with how handsome and imposing he looked in his dark suit. Ashleigh's father had always worn his hair long. Today he had it pulled away from his face in a tight ponytail that accented his high cheekbones and dramatically chiseled features.

The audience was quiet and attentive as the principal introduced Mr. White Eagle.

When Ashleigh's father stood up, he looked calmly around the room. Then his handsome face split into a wide smile.

"It's a real privilege for me to be here today," he began. "First of all, I'm honored to be kicking off the Native American Studies program at the community college in Cedar River. I've been hearing about Cedar River for over a year now. I felt it was time for me to check out this marvelous place that my friends, Jim, Marilyn, and Lexi Leighton, have been talking about so much. I suppose by now most of you have met or seen my daughter, Ashleigh. Normally, Ashleigh doesn't see me at work, so it's a special pleasure to have her in my audience as well."

Several students were glancing furtively between Ashleigh and her father.

"As a Lakota Sioux, I feel that programs like the one being introduced at the college are sorely needed in our country today. Everyone benefits from an acquaintance with his heritage, his history, the place from which he came. Here in America, for Native Americans, our past is your past.

"I see the Native American Studies program here in Cedar River as a forum for friendship, understanding, cooperation, and learning.

"What I'd really like to do today is tell you a few family stories. You all have them, don't you? You've heard your folks start a story by saying, 'When I was your age . . .' "

Several of the kids in the audience nodded.

"You probably felt like rolling your eyes and saying, 'Oh, no, here we go again.' But, if you took the time to really listen, you'd find yourself caught up in the story, genuinely interested in the experiences of another generation. Am I right?"

A few more nodded their heads.

"That's all I'm here to do—to tell you stories about my grandparents, their grandparents, and the grandparents before them—generations of family stories. If you really listen and can imagine the people involved, they'll become quite real to you. Perhaps then you'll view my ancestors with new understanding and compassion. Best of all, perhaps you'll begin to identify with them.

"Now, if you'll bear with me for just a few minutes, I'd like to begin with a story about . . ."

———

Lexi had forgotten what a marvelous storyteller Mr. White Eagle was. He regaled them for nearly an hour with stories about his people, their traditions and beliefs. Everyone was entranced. Lexi felt a warm feeling of satisfaction as she looked around the room. They were listening with rapt attention and new respect. This wasn't an easy crowd to win over, but Mr. White Eagle had done it. In doing so, he'd opened some new windows on history.

With a pang of disappointment, Lexi realized that Mr. White Eagle was looking at his watch. "I'd like to thank you students for your attention. You're a great audience. I encourage each and every one of you to take some time to stop at the college and look through the new additions to the library. There's a marvelous selection of history books to be utilized in the Native American Studies program. Perhaps some of you will even get a taste of it in your high-school classes." He winked at Mr. Raddis. "One of your history teachers has promised that he'll be doing a unit on Native Americans before the year's out."

The dismissal bell rang, and as the kids poured out of the bleachers, several of them came to talk to Mr. White Eagle. A few introduced themselves to Ashleigh as she stood near her father.

Lexi felt a mixture of pleasure and relief for her friend. Maybe the trip would end on a happy note yet!

Chapter Ten

"I can't believe it's almost time for you to go home," Lexi groaned. "It seems like you just got here." The girls were sitting in the living room with Dr. and Mrs. Leighton.

"I know. In some ways this visit has gone too quickly. In others, it seems I've been here forever. A lot has happened."

Lexi turned to her parents. "You should have heard Mr. White Eagle's speech. It was wonderful."

"It *was* good," Ashleigh said proudly. "It almost canceled out the mess with Tim Anders' father and that horrible business with Rita Leonard and her locket."

Lexi groaned and put a pillow over her face. "I am *so* sorry for that," she said with a muffled voice. She pulled the pillow away and looked at Ashleigh in dismay. "I don't even want to think about what happened with Rita and Mr. Anders. I hope you can forget those hateful things they said."

"Well, it worked out, at least with Rita. Todd found her locket. I just keep hoping that my being here made a difference for someone. I've lived in Grover's Point all my life, where we never talked about prejudice. Here, where I'm new and different, the subject just kept coming up. I'd like to feel that maybe I've let one person know that prejudice is just plain wrong. When that kind of mud gets thrown, it stains the one who throws it far more than it ever does the target."

"You're a very sensible girl, Ashleigh," Dr. Leighton commented. "You've come to a very mature realization. After all, racism is based on fear."

"Dad, I still don't get the fear part."

"A racist might say he's not afraid, but he is," Dr. Leighton assured Lexi. "He's afraid of someone who is different from himself. That fear is similar to the fear some people have of Ben."

"Who in the world would be afraid of Ben?" Ashleigh blurted.

"Lots of people—before they get to know him," Lexi answered.

Mrs. Leighton finished answering Ashleigh's question, "Because Ben looks a little different with his classic Down's syndrome features, and because his behavior and development are slower than other boys his age, people are wary of him. They don't know what to say to him or how to act when he's around. In the back of their minds they're just a little worried that some of Ben's handicap might rub off on them. Perhaps they're afraid that someday they may have a child like Ben in their own family. That fear permeates the way they treat Ben." A smile touched Mrs. Leighton's lips. "Of course, once they get to know Ben, things change."

"Ben is such a little honey. I love him," Ashleigh said.

"He is a sweetheart. He's lovable, funny, affectionate, and in many ways, the most charming person in our family."

"Once you get to know Ben," Lexi added, "it changes your idea forever about Down's syndrome children. You begin to realize that they have their own personality, their own quirks, and their own positive attributes."

"And they aren't so frightening anymore," Mrs. Leighton concluded.

"It's too bad that's such a hard lesson to learn," Ashleigh commented. "People miss a lot if they don't know Ben or someone like him."

"At least something can be done about that," Mrs. Leighton said.

"What do you mean, Mom?"

"Prejudice isn't something that we're born with. It's not in our genetic code. We don't *have* to be prejudiced. Children learn prejudice. Babies aren't born hating anyone. They're *taught* to hate.

"Therefore, if we can ever teach one generation not to fear or hate others who are different from themselves, then the next generation will be even less likely to do so."

"And the generation that follows will be even more accepting," Lexi concluded.

"It's a great idea, but I don't see how it can happen," Ashleigh said frankly. "My dad thinks the same way you do, Mrs. Leighton, but it seems like an impossible job to me."

"One person can't change the world all by himself," Mrs. Leighton agreed. "But if each person makes an effort to encourage love and acceptance instead of hatred, that will help."

Mrs. Leighton smiled. "I'm sorry, Ashleigh. We've started a terribly serious conversation. I'm afraid you're going to go home remembering only the somber things."

"Do you know what I'll remember most?"

"I can't imagine. What will it be?"

"Lexi's friends." Ashleigh gave Lexi a coy look. "I think Todd is an absolute doll."

"Of course," Lexi said complacently, a grin on her face.

"But probably the best things are the McNaughton stories."

Even Dr. Leighton chuckled. "Ah, yes, McNaughton stories. I've heard many of them."

"They're going to be a riot to tell at home. No one is going to believe what I tell them about the Chinese dinner we had at their house." Ashleigh's smile wavered. "There's really only one thing that I would change if I could."

Lexi knew immediately what Ashleigh was talking about—*Tim*.

Mrs. Leighton said, "All I can say, Ashleigh, is that I'm very proud of you. You've grown into a fine young woman. I'm glad you're my daughter's friend."

At that moment, Ben came barreling into the room. He paused in the doorway. When his eyes settled on Ashleigh, he broke into a big smile, shot across the room, hiked himself onto the couch, and cuddled up next to her.

"I love you, Ashleigh," he announced. "I'm going to miss you when you're gone. Could you come and live with us?"

"Why, Benjamin, that's the sweetest offer I've had in ages. But I think my parents would be lonely without me, don't you?"

"Maybe," Ben said doubtfully. "But I want you here." He curled his hand into a fist and placed it inside Ashleigh's palm. "If you can't live here, will you play with me anyway?"

"How do you ever say no to this kid?" Ashleigh asked Lexi.

"It's hard." Lexi shrugged helplessly. "Ben's an expert at getting what he wants."

"I want to do a puzzle." Ben darted a look at Ashleigh. "A big puzzle."

"You can set up the card table in here," Mrs. Leighton said. "If I know Ben, he'll pick the largest puzzle we have in the house and it will take the entire family a week to get it together."

Ben had gone for his puzzle when the doorbell rang. "Were you girls expecting someone?" Dr. Leighton asked.

"I don't think so," Lexi said. "We talked to everyone at school. They all had plans for tonight."

"I wonder who it is," Mrs. Leighton said.

Dr. Leighton walked to the front door and opened it. Lexi heard a man's voice asking for Ashleigh White Eagle.

Both girls were shocked to see Mr. Anders walk into the living room. Lexi was stunned by his appearance. For a big man, he looked small tonight. His shoulders were stooped and he wore a worried expression. His face was flushed. Beads of sweat stood on his temple.

"I'm sorry to intrude, but I need to talk to Ashleigh."

What is he doing here? Can't he leave Ashleigh alone?

Lexi saw her parents move closer to Ashleigh's side. No one offered to leave the room as Mr. Anders began to speak.

"This is very difficult for me, you know," he said bluntly.

Ashleigh remained silent.

"I've had a bad weekend with my son."

Lexi felt frozen inside.

"Quite frankly, Tim has hardly spoken to me. When we pass each other in the hallway, he won't look at me. At meal times, he hardly eats and he won't speak. When I confronted him, Tim said some things to me that hurt me deeply."

"I'm not sure we should continue . . ." Dr. Leighton began.

"Please allow me to do this. My son told me that I was unfair, prejudiced, and cruel," Mr. Anders admitted. "It made me very angry at first, but I've had some time to think. I resented my son's hostility. I felt betrayed." He looked at Ashleigh. "And I felt it was all because of you."

"But, sir . . ."

"Let me finish," Mr. Anders insisted. "I've been out of my mind with worry. I love my son. I don't want anything to come between us that might ruin our relationship. Finally, after too much fretting and stewing, I discussed this situation with my brother, a teacher at the college."

"And?" Dr. Leighton said softly.

"My brother suggested that I drive out to the college and listen to Mr. White Eagle's presentation. My brother's in the science department, but the entire college has been very aware of White Eagle's presence on campus. Frankly, I didn't like the idea. I didn't want to hear what this girl's father might say, but I decided that I should do that much to attempt to understand my son.

"I went out there planning to listen to one brief presentation." Mr. Anders laughed sourly. "Instead of one presentation, I ended up hearing all of them. Today, my brother asked me to have lunch with him at the college. Much to my surprise, Mr. White Eagle was a part of the luncheon group."

"You met my father?" Ashleigh gasped.

"If you think you're surprised, imagine how I felt," Mr. Anders said grimly. "I'll have to admit I learned some things that shocked me."

"Such as?" Dr. Leighton was still standing very close to Ashleigh.

"First of all, I learned that *Mr.* White Eagle is actually *Doctor* White Eagle."

"Dad has always felt that people are more comfortable with him if he doesn't use his title. It's not like he's a medical doctor, a dentist, or a veterinarian, like you, Dr. Leighton."

"I've always thought your father underestimates the Ph.D. he holds in history," Dr. Leighton responded. "But your father is a very modest man."

"Modest indeed," Mr. Anders agreed. "I also learned that Dr. White Eagle is a big fan of professional basketball, despises hunting, and his favorite hobby is painting watercolors and oils in his spare time."

Marilyn Leighton nodded. "Richard is very talented artistically. We took a few art classes together when we lived in Grover's Point."

"But what does this have to do with me?" Ashleigh asked.

"Having lunch with your father showed me things that I'd never known before. I realized that all my preconceived notions about him were wrong.

In my mind, I'd convinced myself that your Indian father was probably uneducated, rough, unsophisticated. The term *Indian* told me he must be an outdoorsman who liked to hunt. I believed all the stereotypes."

Ashleigh smiled tightly. "There aren't a lot of buffalo around Grover's Point, sir."

"I never anticipated that he'd be an artist as well. As we talked, I saw that your father was intelligent and charming. After lunch, I asked him if he'd be willing to visit alone with me for a few moments."

"And you told him about what happened?" Ashleigh was shocked.

"I told him. Although I was very ashamed of myself when I did."

"What did he say?"

"Frankly, I wouldn't have been surprised if he'd punched me in the face," Mr. Anders said grimly. "I'd treated you very badly."

"My dad wouldn't do that."

"I know that now. In fact, he was very kind and understanding. He told me that lack of knowledge was something he ran into all the time. He said that although he wasn't happy to hear how I had behaved, he gave me credit for loving my son enough to try to understand him. He recognized how difficult it had been for me to go to the college, to listen to him speak. He gave me more credit than I deserved." Mr. Anders looked as though he wished he could sink through the floor and disappear.

Mr. Anders coughed and shifted his weight from one foot to the other. "That's the reason I've come to apologize. I behaved very badly. I'm sorry. My son Tim was right and I was wrong. Tim is the one with the common sense and good taste. I behaved like a fool."

Ashleigh stared at Mr. Anders dumbfoundedly.

He extended his hand. "My prejudice almost prevented me from getting to know one of the finest, most intelligent people I've ever met, Ashleigh. That person is your father. I would be proud to have my son get to know any child of his. I had no right to judge you without knowing you. I was looking only at the color of your skin. I didn't see or understand your beauty, either inside or out. If you can forgive me, I'd be very grateful."

Lexi could feel tears stinging her eyes. She knew how much it had taken for Mr. Anders to come here tonight and she was deeply impressed by his sincere apology.

"Of course I forgive you," Ashleigh said matter-of-factly.

Mr. Anders took a handkerchief out of his pocket and mopped his brow. "I hope you don't mind," he continued. "I suppose I've overstepped my boundaries again, but I told my son that if you weren't too angry and would be willing to accept an invitation from me, I'd like to treat you, Tim, Lexi, and Todd to that dinner at The Station.

"You don't have to do that, Mr. Anders," Ashleigh said."

"I know I don't have to. I *want* to. I feel like I've been hovering on the brink of disaster all weekend. Not only was I in danger of losing my son, but I also almost lost a chance to meet some really fine people. You'd be doing me a great favor if you'd accept."

"Well, of course, if you really want us to."

"You've made me a very happy man." Mr. Anders

laughed shakily. "If you wouldn't mind, I'd appreciate it if you'd call Tim. He's at home wondering what's happening here tonight."

"Poor Tim!" Ashleigh gasped. I'll call him right now."

"Please." Mr. Anders held out his hand and stopped Ashleigh as she turned to go. "There's something else I want to tell you. I was at church on Sunday and I heard your song . . . that's really when it happened. Something spoke to me through your music. It was as if I could see how wrong I'd been and how desperately I needed to make amends."

Suddenly Lexi felt as though she were going to burst with joy. A smile of satisfaction slid across her face. That wasn't *something* speaking to Mr. Anders, Lexi was sure of it. That was *Someone!*

All in all, it was the perfect note on which to end Ashleigh's visit to Cedar River.

BOOK #19

In book #19, Todd's brother, Mike, can't keep up with the workload at his garage now that he has a girlfriend to occupy his time. When Mike hires Ed, he seems like the answer to his prayers. He's hard-working and very reliable. But Ed is hiding something. Will Lexi and Todd be able to uncover the secret that Ed is so determined to keep?

A Note From Judy

I'm glad you're reading *Cedar River Daydreams*!
I hope I've given you something to think about as
well as a story to entertain you. If you feel you have
any of the problems that Lexi and her friends experience, I encourage you to talk with your parents, a
pastor, or a trusted adult friend. There are many people who care about you!

I love to hear from my readers, so if you'd like to
receive my newsletter and a bookmark, please send
a self-addressed, stamped envelope to:

Judy Baer
Bethany House Publishers
6820 Auto Club Road
Minneapolis, MN 55438